CHILD
OF ALL
NATIONS

CHILD OF ALL NATIONS

IRMGARD KEUN

Translated from the German by Michael Hofmann

THE OVERLOOK PRESS
Woodstock & New York

This edition first published in the United States in 2008 by
The Overlook Press, Peter Mayer Publishers, Inc.
Woodstock & New York

WOODSTOCK:
One Overlook Drive
Woodstock, NY 12498
www.overlookpress.com
[for individual orders, bulk and special sales, contact our Woodstock office]

NEW YORK:
141 Wooster Street
New York, NY 10012

Cataloging-in-Publication Data is available from the Library of Congress

Manufactured in the United States of America
ISBN 978-1-59020-099-5
10 9 8 7 6 5 4 3 2 1

The translator would like to thank the antique bookseller Christoph Hoffmeister (himself no antique) for the introduction to Keun, and Jakob Hofmann, then thirteen, this translation's first reader and editor.

M. H.

CHILD
OF ALL
NATIONS

I get funny looks from hotel managers, but that's not because I'm naughty; it's the fault of my father. Everyone says: that man ought never to have got married.

At first they treat me as if I was a rich lady's Pekinese. The chambermaids make kissy mouths at me and little *mwah mwah* noises. The maître d' slips me postage stamps, which I save, because I might be able to sell them later. The man in the lift lets me press the button to our floor, and he doesn't interfere, much. And the waiters brandish table-napkins at me in a friendly sort of way. But all that comes to an end when my father has to leave to raise money, and my mother and me are left behind, and the bill still hasn't been paid. We are left behind as surety, and my father says we've got as much riding on us as if we'd been fur coats or diamonds.

Then the waiters in the hotel restaurant no longer brandish their napkins in that jolly way; instead they flick them at our table. Mama says they do it to clear the crumbs away, but it looks to me more like what you do to keep away pesky cats that have their eyes on the roast.

We hardly dare go to the restaurant any more, Mama and me. But there's nowhere else we can go, if we're not to starve. Because we haven't got a single franc left, and can't afford to buy any more cheap cheese or apples or bread to sneak up to our room.

My father took all our money with him on his journey to Prague. 'Eat and drink. You've got credit here, don't worry about a thing – I've got it all sorted out,' is what he said as he stood on the railway platform in Brussels. We were wearing our thin coats, because they were the warmest we had. We felt cold and worried as we kissed him goodbye. His fair hair blew about in a laughing sort of way as he leaned out of the window and waved back at us. Mama cried.

In the hotel restaurant my mother doesn't dare order anything cheap, because that doesn't go down well with waiters, and we can't afford to irritate people even more than we have been doing anyway. We've stopped taking the lift as well, because we can't give tips, and we always rush past the porters. We don't hand in our room key either, because we don't want to spend a single second in front of the desk, and the maître d' has stopped giving me stamps too. My mother says his face looks more like a final demand to her than a human face.

My father's been gone a week – we don't know where

he is, he hasn't managed to write to us yet. Three days ago, though, I got a parcel from him from Budapest, because it was my birthday. I was ten. Maybe my father sent me a doll or an embroidered dress, but we don't know what it is, because there was duty to pay on the parcel, so we couldn't afford to collect it. My mother didn't want to borrow the money from the maître d'; she's not good at that sort of thing. My father's better. Once he even borrowed a hundred francs from a postman. It's an awful thing if a parcel comes, and you can't even open it to see what's inside. It's my parcel, but I can't get at it. Still, it looks like we'll be in Belgium for a while, so maybe I can get it later.

My father always manages to get hold of money from somewhere. And he always comes back to us too. I don't think he ever completely forgets about us. That time in Ostende he didn't forget about me completely either, but he nearly did.

It was summer 1936 that we were in Ostende. I found loads of pretty shells, and starfish, and little baby crabs, and I made an aquarium out of them. But I wasn't supposed to take it to Brussels, because I was travelling with a large doll's kitchen and a toy grocery store and a couple of tortoises, as it was.

At first in Ostende I didn't have any other children to play with, because they spoke French and I couldn't understand them. I only speak German, and most of that is actually Kölsch.a

We left Germany when my father couldn't stand it any more, because he writes books and articles for newspapers. We emigrated to find freedom. We're never going to go back to Germany. Anyway, we don't need to, because the world is a very big place.

Most of my father's money from books is in Holland, but that's almost irrelevant, because he's usually spent it before it arrives. So my father says he has to come up with other connections and sources of money. My mother and I are a burden on my father, but seeing as he's got us, he means to keep us.

'My plump little goldfinch,' he says to my mother, because she's got flyaway golden hair, a round soft bosom like a bird's and frightened eyes, and she always looks as though she's on the point of flying away. She doesn't seem to sit firmly and heavily, the way people usually sit; she perches nervously like a bird on a twig.

I look a lot like my mother, only she has bluer eyes than me, and bigger legs, and she's bigger all round. She wears her hair combed back, and in a knot at the back of her head. My hair is short and unruly. My mother's much prettier than I am, but I don't cry so much.

*

* Dialect of German spoken in Cologne. (Trans.)

Ostende has one fancy beach and a smaller, cheaper one for people of slenderer means. In either case, you don't get the use of the sea for nothing; at most you're allowed to gaze at it, like the passing clouds in the sky. I'd love to lie on a cloud one day, but you can only do that when you're dead. You can go in the sea when you're alive, but you need money. At least, that's the way it was in Ostende. Probably you are allowed to go in the water, but only in your clothes, and only as far in as you can lift them. Of course, that's not much use, because you can't pick up a dress very far; it's not respectable. Because we wanted to go into the water respectably without our clothes and up to our necks, we put my father to expense. He thinks bathing is unhealthy. In Ostende he preferred to sit in a café on the beach, where he drank something brown that tasted really nasty and isn't even supposed to be on sale in Belgium.

My father also said he didn't like Brussels, because of the poor standard of drinks there. But they have wonderful things that I've never tasted before. Sweet juices made out of exotic fruits like pineapple and grapefruit.

My father writes for our living. In Ostende he was working on a new book, but he couldn't finish it, because we had too many worries. When my mother and me went to collect my father at lunchtime, his eyes sometimes looked as if they had swum far out to sea and weren't completely back yet. My mother and I are both very good swimmers, but my father's eyes swim much further than either of us. Often he would send us away again, because he didn't want to eat anything. A settled life makes it impossible for him to work, and the thought of it disgusts him. We only eat once a day, because that's cheaper, and it's perfectly adequate. I'm always hungry anyway, even if I eat seven times a day.

We treated ourselves to the fancy beach once, where you get changed in a castle where the walls and floors are of shiny gems, and little fountains pop up like leaping flowers. But the fancy beach is just as dirty as the inexpensive one, and it doesn't have any more shells either. Every morning my mother would lie in the sun on the poor people's beach with pieces of orange peel on her skin. Her skin got to be like brown velvet.

Sometimes aeroplanes would hum over our heads, very heavy and droning. I wished one might fall down – even though the thought of that scared me. Thank God it didn't happen. Big ships sailed out of the port to go to England. I often used to stand and wave to them. What I liked best were the white sailing boats, because they looked like the little pair of butterfly wings my grandmother owns. She has them on her sewing-box, where they're held by a little blue prince.

Sometimes I'd be scared my mother might be trampled to death, because the small beach was so crammed with balls and people and dogs chasing back and forth. Once, my mother was picked up and tossed by a wave, but I never was.

I played in the water and touched the waves. At first they feel ghastly cold, but they end up making me feel warmer than the sun. Once I kicked a pale-blue jellyfish in two, because of the way it sparkled, and because I felt like destroying something, and also I wanted there suddenly to be lots and lots of jellyfish. Then I spat into the sea and watched my spit floating, and I felt ashamed of myself and thought I'd dirtied the sea. But then a wave washed over my spit, and it was gone.

I unscrewed a wheel from a really old bathing cart so that I could play at surfing and do proper cartwheels. The wheel was almost coming off by itself. Three other children helped me. While we were working together, I suddenly learned French, and we all made excited noises together. I was too excited to feel embarrassed in front of the other children, and all at once I could speak as well as they could. '*Ça va?*' they said. '*Ça va, ça va!*' I shouted back. Now I know more French words than I can count. I don't know what they all mean, but that doesn't matter.

So Belgian children can play as well. We stuck the wheel in the sand and arranged shells between the spokes and seaweed, and sang, '*Allez allez au bon marché*'. Lots of children came and bought shells that they paid for with other shells. And the big horses that pull the bathing carts trotted round about us. They didn't step on anything.

There was trouble later on, because my father had to

pay for the wheel, after some great waves came and washed it away. My father was terribly strict. He said I would be the ruin of the whole family, and it was up to me to be twice and thrice as good, so that I made a good impression in a foreign country. Even though I know you make a much better impression in a foreign country if you aren't so terribly good. But of course grown-ups aren't going to know that, because they don't spend their time playing with foreign children.

I cried over the wheel, and my father had to comfort me and take me along to the Renommée. The Renommée is a wonderful restaurant, and so hideously expensive that the waiters outnumber the diners. (They're better dressed than the diners, too.) The walls are covered with mirrors and the tablecloths are so starched and white that I was afraid to look at them for fear they might get dirty. There are lots of glasses and flowers on the tables, and the napkins are built up into little towers. I prefer tables where they leave you some elbow room. But my father had to eat some special caviar and drink a bottle of some special champagne, because he felt bad; and that's why he took me there.

My father felt bad because he hadn't eaten anything for several days on account of his money worries, and because he had been telephoning round foreign cities without success. That morning he had said: 'That's it now, I have lost all hope.' He had borrowed another hundred francs from the porter, who is a friend of his, and with that he could pay what he owed in the café at the Place d'Armes, where he always goes to work in the afternoons. At lunchtime he had to go back to the porter to borrow more money to pay for my bathing-cart wheel that was washed away.

Then my father suddenly walked into our hotel room where I was crying and my mother was groaning, and said to my mother: 'Well, a miracle has happened – it might yet save us. I've just had a call from Tulpe. You don't know him; well, I don't know him either, I crossed paths with him once in Berlin. He reads my books, heard I was in town, called me. He travels in ladies' underwear, I believe; probably has a bank account – rock-solid character. Two thousand francs will be enough to get us out of trouble. I can pay him back with the rights to the Polish translation; the money for that is due in the next few weeks. Then I send the publishers a hundred pages in Amsterdam – when will you have a moment to type them? We'll stand to get three hundred guilders. I'm meeting the man at six, I'll call you in the hotel at eight – I feel so ill, everything is so disgusting, the man is bound to be sticky. I have to go and prepare myself for the meeting, gather my strength, get myself into the right frame of mind. Give me a kiss – no, don't. Eight o'clock then – why is she crying like that? I'll take her along.'

In the Renommée I was allowed to eat wild strawberries with whipped cream and drink real coffee with just a *soupçon* of milk in it, like grown-ups do. My father ate caviar, which I don't like because it has a fishy taste, and he drank two bottles of champagne. After that he felt better, and went off. 'Wait for me here,' he said to me. 'I'm just getting some money to pay the bill. I'll be back in an hour – tell the waiter you want an ice cream, or would you rather have a piece of cake instead?'

I had a dish of ice cream and waited, and my father didn't come. I felt terribly bored; out of petulance I ate some cake, and waited a bit longer. Once, a cat sat down next to me, a grey cat; I petted her. I was all alone in the restaurant; the waiter came along one time and gave my table a brush. I wondered what everything cost in the restaurant, and whether one naughty girl would be enough to pay for it.

The skies outside turned red. My mother always says: the angels are laughing. But I wasn't in a mood for laughing, and my mother couldn't find me. She didn't know where I was. She had an assignation with Frau Fiedler in the big Café Wellington.

We know Frau Fiedler because her husband is another penniless writer. I don't like Herr Fiedler, because he once said to my parents in the café on the Place d'Armes: 'Thank God we don't have any children ourselves.' Maybe he thinks my parents should just throw me away. I think that was mean of him. He often buys me ice-cream cones. He always tries to pat me on the head. I eat his ice cream, but when he tries to pat my head, I push him away.

I no longer knew what to do. How long does a child have to sit still for in order to pay a bill? I sat on a green sofa covered in stiff, ridged material. My father kept not coming; I thought I might have to spend the night all alone on the sofa. With that I would have paid all our debts, and could leave in the morning. We would be saved.

The lights were turned on, all at once it was raining light. The waiters rigged up a Christmas table in the middle of the restaurant. Thousands of crates of light wood were piled up, containing peaches and grapes and apples, and thousands of dishes were put out, full of brown and green and white sauces for things to swim around in. Also there were chicken legs made into jelly-fish, and lots of horrid things for grown-ups, hams and terribly long sausages, peas and flowers.

I got up from my place and walked round the Christmas display. I kept getting in the way of the waiters. I identified an apricot I would have liked to try. But I didn't touch it, because I knew all that costs money. It was only at my grandmother's that you could have things for free, and that's a long time ago now.

A woman turned up who was gaudy and glittery and laughed a lot. A serious dark man swarmed all over her like an octopus, three distinguished waiters ran up to her with bent backs and drove her back on to a sofa. The table was moved out – the couple shuffled round it and sat down. Waiters moved the table back so that the couple couldn't get off the sofa: they were trapped.

More diners arrived. I couldn't stand to watch any more, yet I couldn't go to sleep on my sofa either. Some waiters took me to the cloakroom. They talked to me, but I couldn't understand them. One of them knew German, but I didn't understand him. I tried my French, but they couldn't understand that, clearly because they weren't children. I just understood 'Papa'. So I too said 'Papa'. And then we all said 'Papa' together.

I was seated at a small table. Behind me the waiters were clinking around with knives and forks, next to me a woman in black sat at the till and twiddled around with it. I was so tired I didn't know which I wanted more, to sleep or cry. Then a waiter gave me an apple. I would have preferred my apricot, because apricots are soft and not so strenuous to eat. As I ate the apple, I suddenly had to cry and fall asleep.

I didn't notice how someone carried me into the cloakroom. I suppose it's a miracle my father found me, because he didn't give up a hat or coat and so didn't have a cloakroom ticket. All at once he was there, kissing me and exclaiming: 'Did you really think your father would have forgotten all about you?'

I said, 'Yes.'

'Can you understand how a man might live for something like that, Herr Tulpe?' asked my father. A little dark-haired man drilled his fingers in my hair, which I don't like. There was another man there as well, who said: 'I think it's best to let sleeping children lie.'

'But it's only nine o'clock,' said my father, and paid the bill so that I could go back to my mother. As we left, a waiter said, *'Au revoir, mademoiselle'* to me.

We went to the café on the Place d'Armes, where I was allowed to spend ten francs on the slot machine. But I didn't get any benefit from it, because I wasn't allowed to turn the crank myself. My father always cranked, and it's the cranking that's the fun of it. Machines like that are the greatest thing. A thousand presents are hidden behind glass in little green baubles. Over them is a crane with a pair of mechanical claws. You have to put a franc in the machine to move the crane and pick out a present with its claws, which it hardly ever does, because they're mostly too low for it to reach. The claws have hardly any strength in them either; it can drive you wild.

At ten my mother came along. She was crying because I'd been lost and my father hadn't called. She said his thoughtlessness bordered on callousness. She didn't want to have a go at the machine either, she just wanted to take me straight home to bed.

My father squeezed us into a taxi. I was thinking, we could easily have walked home and saved the fare. The taxi driver couldn't leave because my father was still standing on the pavement. He was holding the hand of my mother, who was sitting next to me on the dark taxi seat. The music was loud on the Place d'Armes, a little boy kept going round the bandstand on a scooter; there were lots of little children sitting on the pavement who were smaller than I was. They didn't have to go to bed yet.

My father was saying to my mother: 'I'll tell you everything later. I've got a little money – don't ask, it was ghastly. Poor Tulpe is having an awful time of it – delightful chap by the way, you'll meet him soon. It turns out he was hoping for money from me; thank God I could help him out. That saved his bacon. At that point he remembered he knew a man by the name of Max Popp who lives in Brussels and sometimes comes to Ostende for weekends. What he does then is sit on the pier by your beach and breathe in the healthful sea air, poor devil. Apart from that, he's not a bad man.

'Thank God we ran into Popp on the pier. He used to own a calendar factory in Thuringia, but now he's living in Brussels. There's something a little repulsive about him, but you get used to it. He doesn't take his drink too well. The red rash is apparently something he picked up at the barber's. Makes him a bit shy of being introduced to you. He has a most exquisite girlfriend, very delicate, with a lovely face – ow, why did you pull your hand away like that? You scratched me! I'd like to give her a little present tomorrow before she leaves, I've no idea what – will you turn your mind to it, Annie? Maybe you'll think of something.

'I'm just dictating Popp some of my advertising concepts – you know, if something like that comes off, we suddenly stand to make a lot of money. Popp has connections with department stores in Paris and Brussels, and offers them advertising concepts.

'He lives in a tiny rundown hotel. He's bound to have money – only rich people live as frugally as that. Tulpe didn't think it was possible that he would come good. Will you excuse me the details now, Annie, I have to go back to the café. And at eleven I'm meeting Monsieur Corbet, our nice porter. A sweet fellow, a real gentleman, and fond of a drink. I asked him out to an Italian restaurant for a good bottle of wine. I think it's best not to introduce Popp and Tulpe to him.'

My mother wanted the driver to set off, because it's awfully expensive to keep a lady idling in a taxi. It's much more than if it's just a man. My mother is always cross about the expense when my father gives a man friend a lift home in a taxi, and she has a bit of a fit. But when my father gives a woman friend a lift home in a taxi, then my mother doesn't say anything at all. Even though that upsets her much more.

We drove slowly along the Rue de la Chapelle to the port area, where we were staying in a nice hotel – not a shabby little one like Herr Popp. My mother would have preferred to stay on the beach in a little pension, but my father is always set on a proper hotel, where he doesn't have to take his meals, and where there are porters who will write and deliver letters for him, even though my mother always offers to type for him. That's why we have our very own typewriter, even though it was very expensive, and only broke down once, after I secretly practised on it.

But my father almost never asks my mother to type for him. One time he said to her: 'If a man lives with a woman, he shouldn't have her working for him. She always imagines she's suffering anyway. And so he can't get nervous, or be annoyed about her mistakes or even be matter of fact with her, but only ever respond with gratitude and emotion, and I don't feel like that. It even bothers me when you sew on a button for me, Annie. Frankly I'd rather have the chambermaid do it. She'll do it better, and she'll be happy with a tip, and I can be friendly to her and say thank you, without her coming over all moved and hurling herself at me or bursting into tears. Oh, if only you'd let me do more for you.'

'You're very unfair,' said my mother.

'Maybe so,' said my father, 'but save me from the ministrations of solicitous females.'

During this scene, we were sitting in a little café by the port. Women pushed carts of prawns and smooth flat fish that smelled nasty and dripped pale blood. The fish were hung up next to us, like items of laundry out to dry. Fishermen walked over the beach. They wore reddish-yellow jackets – the house of my grandmother in Cologne is that sort of colour.

There was another café right next door to ours, and beyond that another one. In fact there was a whole line of these little cafés: in front of them were little tables for visitors and little stalls with heaps and heaps of sea creatures. Opposite us, but not too near, was the black railway station. A breeze carried the smells of the locomotives to where we were sitting. The hanging fish stirred, the sky trembled slightly, and was very blue. My scalp felt chilly because my hair was still damp after swimming; my mother's hair was still wet as well.

Mama looked as if she'd spent a long time sitting out in the rain. She had unmoving sad eyes. Slowly she raised her hand to clutch the air, then let it fall heavily in her lap.

I drank fizzy water, which tickled my nose, and bumped glasses with my mother, but she never even noticed. She'd ordered five langoustines. And now she wasn't eating them. My father picked up one of the pink langoustines and slowly, without speaking, removed one of its black button eyes. I thought that was disgusting.

'Don't you love me any more?' asked my mother. Thereupon she pulled out the langoustine's other eye, and I ran off because a tiny little white puppy was running around on the street. I wanted to stroke it and play with it, and above all save it from the big trucks that were driving past all the time.

I wished the little puppy didn't belong to anyone. That was stupid of me, of course. Everything cute belongs to someone. The puppy belonged to the newspaper seller who keeps shouting out: '*Écho de Paris!*' Later, I was able to visit the puppy at his house.

My parents called me because they wanted to go. My father paid for the langoustines, even though there were still some left on the plate. My mother seized my hand and marched down the uneven pavement with me. My father dawdled along behind us – we kept turning round to check, and then he walked even more slowly.

Sometimes my father loves us, and sometimes he doesn't. When he doesn't, we can't do anything about it, my mother and me. Nothing is any good when he doesn't love us. Then we're not allowed to cry in his presence or laugh, we mustn't give him anything, or take anything from him either. Any steps we might take only have the effect of delaying even more the time when he will love us again. Because he always comes back to us. We just have to hold still and wait, and then everything takes care of itself. There's nothing else we can do anyway.

My mother spends more time waiting than I do, because she doesn't play much, and she has no little friends. Now we're in Brussels, waiting for my father. That's what our life is like. It's always terribly hard to move to a new city, and we almost didn't make it to Brussels either.

There were almost no summer visitors left in Ostende. There was an English boy I knew, but he had already gone. We couldn't go swimming any more, the sea had grown gigantically wild. The clouds came down from the sky, and the waves climbed up to the clouds. When my mother and I wanted to go for walks on the dike like before, the wind kept us pinned to the spot.

The bellboy from our hotel was going on holiday so we could use the loos in the hotel restaurant for nothing, because the toilet lady had gone as well. Marguerite had gone to her boyfriend, who would keep her warm. She was the one who tidied up our rooms, and sewed on my father's buttons, and sometimes said to my mother: 'I feel sorry for all women.' When I was alone and crying, she went and sat by me sometimes and cried and wrote letters to a French soldier at my father's desk. She said he wasn't a soldier, but an officer. I asked my father about that, and he said it was a mistake. An officer was a soldier too. I told Marguerite that, and she was cross with me. Other than that, she was always kind.

When no more visitors came, she left the hotel to be with her boyfriend, who has a café in Ostende which isn't for foreigners. She came back to visit us once in the hotel, and she was completely different. She didn't have a white lace cap and a black dress or a white apron. She had funny blonde curls and a big black hat. And she was wearing a coloured silk blouse – and you could see that underneath she had big snowballs just like my mother. My mother says those are breasts. I pray to God I never get anything like that growing on me.

★

Without my necklace, we'd never have made it to Brussels. My necklace was so beautiful.

My father often loses money – not banknotes, but they're not proper money anyway. Proper money is round and hard, and being round it often rolls away. The French and the Belgians understood that, and so they drilled a hole through the middle of their centimes. My mother didn't understand what the holes were for, but I did.

Every day I crawled around my father's room collecting the centime pieces. Once I got wedged under the wardrobe. Thank God my feet were still sticking out. Marguerite grabbed me by them and pulled with all her strength. I got a bump on my head, but I was saved. I know there are people who dive in the sea for pearls, which is very dangerous; when I'm grown up I mean to do that too. But, for a child, diving for coins in a carpet is dangerous enough.

I threaded all the centime pieces on a piece of red silk thread. I ended up having three bracelets of them and a necklace that hung down to my belly button. I jingled everywhere I went, and could feel the weight on my shoulders. I felt like one of those bemedalled old men called veterans that they have hanging around guarding the pictures in museums.

One evening we were finally able to pay the hotel bill in Ostende. The manager and manageress both came and kissed us goodbye. That left us with just enough money to get to Brussels third class. But at least that was something.

A chilly breeze blew over the station platform. Our luggage was already in the compartment, including my doll's kitchen and the big box full of shells and rocks and starfish. Errand boys and porters stood around us, making impatient gestures. My father was rummaging around in his pockets. 'Give me some change, will you,' he said to my mother. My mother looked forlornly up at the sky, the bunch of red dahlias in her hand trembled. There was no one we knew anywhere; all the people we knew had left Ostende long ago.

The conductor was already starting to bang the doors shut, when my father beamed all over his face and tore off my chain of office, and we climbed in. Slowly the train rolled away. Like a king, my father tossed the chain out of the window to the porters.

While we were travelling we were happy. My father laughed and kissed us and sang a Cologne song that they sing during Carnival:*9 'It could, it could, it could have been all right . . .'

To begin with, we were happy in Brussels too. We hired a taxi to ferry our luggage. The railway porters were paid by the taxi driver. The taxi driver was paid by the

* Widely and wildly celebrated in Cologne, which is historically a Catholic city. (Trans.)

maître d' at the hotel. Then we greeted the waiters and chambermaids, who remembered us from old times: they were all pleased to see us.

But unfortunately something a bit awful happened upstairs. When my mother came to put me to bed, she suddenly turned very pale, and then I felt sick as well, because there was such a horrible smell. My mother called my father, who said: 'You're right. There is a bad smell. A decomposing corpse, I should say.'

My mother thought someone must have been murdered in the room, and didn't dare open the wardrobe and chest of drawers. My father sniffed the air thoughtfully, then he picked up my cardboard box, which contained all my marine treasures. When he opened it, we all covered our mouths and noses right away. The stones and the shells wouldn't have smelled so bad by themselves, but I'd also included discarded langoustines and dead crabs.

My father was very angry with me. But how was I to know those quiet dead things in their pretty shells would suddenly start to smell so infernally? I don't understand it. Maybe they were still alive and made that smell out of vengefulness. I was so sure they were dead, otherwise I would certainly not have packed them in the box. I wouldn't treat my tortoises like that, so you see I know how to deal with living things.

My father hated me, and I was terribly unhappy. My mother had to empty a whole bottle of Fougère Royale over the box before my father agreed to dash downstairs with it into the dark of Brussels, to dump it unobtrusively somewhere. Then my mother and I sat down in the open window, and waited for the smell to leave the room and my father to come back.

My father came back very late, because he met a policeman on the way. He made friends with the policeman, who helped him hide the package under a park bench, and then the two of them went off together to have a drink. As my father couldn't pay, he had to call the poet Fiedler, who's staying in Brussels for the time being, and who doesn't have any money either. And then Herr Fiedler came along, plus a bookseller who worships my father, and he agreed to lend him seventy francs. My mother and I had fallen asleep sadly in the window when my father made his happy return.

Night was breaking up over the Place Rogier. Through the early morning mist we could see the glowing flowers that the first of the flower-sellers were putting out. We saw a big wooden roof that hadn't been there when we'd arrived. Workmen had spent the night knocking it up. Little beads of damp hung in my mother's blonde hair, making it go even curlier. I was tired, and so was my mother.

My father was standing behind us. 'What are you still doing up at this time?' he asked.

'Are you still cross?' I asked him. 'Mama explained everything to me; I didn't know that dead things can smell so horrible. I never want to smell like that, I want to live for ever.'

My father was standing behind us. He held my face in one hand, and in his other hand he held my mother's. 'You two,' he said, 'you're the dearest things I have in the world.' Then he undressed me and put me to bed. He dragged my mother away to his room. She would have slept much better in my bed, which was much bigger; I was sure of that. I called out after them to tell them, but neither of them seemed to hear me.

'Kully,' my mother said, 'will you telephone downstairs to the concierge to see if a letter's come, ask them to send breakfast up, and then tell me everything you know about Barbarossa?'

My mother is standing in front of her dresser, slowly twisting her hair into a knot. She is wearing a little pink blouse, and she doesn't look anything like a grown-up, but like a girl who's come to play with me. I'm still lying in bed. It feels lovely and warm, and my mother says: 'Who knows how long we'll be able to live like this?'

I take the telephone into bed with me and call downstairs. There's no letter from my father. I order breakfast. Jeanette brings it up, and smiles at us. My mother gives her a silk blouse, because it's been so long that she hasn't been able to give her a tip. At first Jeanette refuses, then finally she agrees to take it.

My mother opens the window. The air is cold, and

it smells somehow Christmassy. On the Beau Marché diagonally across from us, there's a huge shimmering silvery Santa Claus. My mother wants me to eat all the breakfast by myself. We always order one breakfast between two, so that the bill doesn't get even higher. That's the only thing we eat all day. We don't even dare show our faces in the restaurant.

Mama's grown very thin. I think it'll take my father to come back, to make her put on some weight again. 'Get dressed, Kully,' she says, 'and tell me what you know about Barbarossa.' She sits by the window and doesn't even notice that I don't wash behind my ears.

'Barbarossa was an emperor with a long beard,' I say. That's the kind of thing I have to learn. I don't go to school, my mother gives me lessons.

When I was in Germany, before, I did go to school, and that's where I learned to read and write. Then my father didn't want to be in Germany any more, because the government had locked up friends of his, and because he couldn't write or say the things he wanted to write and say. I wonder what the point is of children in Germany still having to learn to read and write?

When my father wanted to leave, my grandmother wanted my mother to come and live with her. But my mother wanted to stay with my father. Then my grandmother wanted me to live with her, but my parents wanted to take me with them, and I wanted to go with them wherever they went.

One time, my mother cried and said: 'But the girl has to learn something; she has to have a proper education, or what's going to become of her?' Then she thought of packing me off to Paris to be with nuns.

My mother cried, and I yelled. And my father said: 'All right, now quiet down, both of you. Kully, stop yelling, you're staying with us.' And then he said to my mother: 'Come on, Annie, leave the girl be. There's no need for her to be any better educated than you are – so why don't you just teach her what you know?'

On the way to the Grande Place there's a little street which is chock-a-block with old bookshops. There my mother found a couple of old German schoolbooks that she uses to teach me geography and history. She couldn't do it without the help of the books, because she's long since forgotten whatever she learned at school, and that can't have been much, it seems to me.

My mother is thirty. When she started going to school, it was wartime. Then what the children mostly learned was to form an orderly crocodile when there was an air raid, and to go down to the bomb shelter in the basement, and also to pack field parcels and make collections for war victims. Other than that, she got lots of days off, because of victorious battles, or because there was no coal, or because everyone was dead from influenza.

I don't know why I'm supposed to learn about things like Barbarossa: it's not as though that'll come in handy in later life, or anything. Even my mother says if you want to use the things you learn at school, you're pretty much restricted to being a teacher. And either you won't have the brains for it, or you'll have starved to death before you become one. And my mother says that of all the things she needed to know in her life, there was not one that she'd learned at school.

My mother has lots of important skills. She knows how to roll cigarettes for my father, which are half the price of ordinary cigarettes. She knows how to remove the inkstains that my father likes to leave in handkerchiefs, and she can pack suitcases so that three times as much goes in them as when my father packs them. He would either have to run out and buy a new suitcase, or else give away anything that won't fit. And then she can do our laundry in the sink in the hotel, and iron it with her little travelling iron, and all without anyone in the hotel noticing. My father mustn't notice either, because he doesn't like her doing that. But he does like it when she knits caps and pullovers for us that we look nice in when we go around in them.

There are lots of other things my mother is good at doing, but she can't peel prawns as fast as I can!

Before, my mother and I used to go for a walk every day for an hour before lunch to have some exercise. Now we don't have lunch, but we still go for a walk so we at least get some fresh air. My mother says it's almost as good for you as eating.

Every day we walk down the Rue Neuve to the Grande Place, because my father used to be so fond of that. It is very nice there too. The big houses gleam in the sun like silver and gold, and the flower stalls have the brightest and most colourful flowers in the world. My mother always wants to see all the flowers. She says she much prefers looking at all of them to buying just a few. But when we have money, we do buy some anyway, because of the enthusiastic way the flower-sellers wave and shout to us.

My mother is very sad as she walks along beside me. She is afraid that I'm hungry, and she is afraid that something might have happened to my father. We can't write to him, we can't send him a wire, and we can't telephone him – we have no address for him at all.

I say to my mother: 'I don't think anything has happened to him,' and then my mother heaves a deep sigh of relief. But she still doesn't know what's to become of us. As we slowly walk along, she doesn't teach me about Barbarossa, instead she talks about our perilous situation. There are apparently so many perils facing us that it's very hard to understand.

Above all, I need to learn what a visa is. We have German passports, which the police gave us in Frankfurt. A passport is a little booklet with stamps in. Basically, it's to prove that you're alive. If you lose your passport, then as far as the whole world is concerned you might as well have died. You're not allowed to go to any more countries. You have to leave the country you're in, but you're not allowed to enter a different one. Unfortunately, God made people in such a way that they have to live on land. I now secretly pray every night that in future people might be able to float in the water for years on end, or fly around in the air.

My mother read to me from the Bible. It says there that God created the world, but it doesn't say anything about borders. You can't cross a border without a passport and a visa. I always wanted to see a border properly for myself, but I've come to the conclusion that you can't. My mother can't explain it to me either. She says: 'A border is what separates one country from another.' At first I thought borders were like fences, as high as the sky. But that was silly of me, because how could trains go through them? Nor can a border be a strip of land either, because then you could just sit down on top of the border, or walk around in it, if you had to leave one country and weren't able to go into the next one. You would just stay on the border, and build yourself a little hut and live there and make faces at the countries on either side of you. But a border has nowhere for you to set your foot. It's a drama that happens in the middle of a train, with the help of actors who are called border guards.

If you have a visa, then the guards let you stay on the train and travel on. Because our passport was issued in Frankfurt, we can only get visas issued in Frankfurt. But

Frankfurt is in Germany, and we can't return to Germany, because then the government would lock us up, ever since my father told the French newspapers and other newspapers, and he even wrote it in a book, about how much he hates the government. A visa is a stamp in your passport. Each country you want to go to, you first have to ask it to give you one of its stamps. And for that you have to go to a consulate. A consulate is an office where you are made to wait quietly for a very long time and be on your best behaviour. A consulate is like a piece of the border in the middle of a different country; the consul is the king of the border.

A principal characteristic of visas is that they expire. To begin with, we're always terribly pleased to get a visa for a different country. But then the visa starts to expire, every day it expires a little more – and finally it's completely expired, and then we have to leave that country. I must learn about all this. Sometimes it makes my mother cry, and she says how it all used to be so much easier before. But I wasn't alive at the time when it was all so much easier.

Anyway, I'm not scared of uniformed policemen or of officials on trains. When we went to Poland, a customs man wanted to take away my doll's kitchen from me, and he wanted not to admit my two tortoises either. In the end, he even let me blow my nose on his handkerchief.

Here in Brussels a traffic policeman on the Place Rogier wanted to arrest me because I walked past the cars at the wrong time and because I stared at the policeman who looked so majestic on his white throne in the middle of the busy traffic. There were changing red and green lights, and I found it a lovely spectacle altogether. You're only supposed to cross the road when the light is on green, but I forget that sometimes, because I like the red light better.

When I looked at the traffic policeman, the traffic stopped and couldn't be controlled any more. It was just as well those cars happened not to want to run me over; there was only one of them that did, but luckily its driver was able to restrain it just in time.

Cars are much more dangerous than lions, and they need to be very carefully controlled because they always feel like charging at people. Lions only do that when they're very hungry. Lions don't scare me at all. I think I would only be very slightly scared if a hungry lion were to charge me. Maybe I would stay just exactly where I was, and talk to him and stroke him. You can't do that with a car if a car charges you; that's why I always run away from charging cars. Because a car would like nothing better than to kill you.

When I was standing in the middle of the traffic, feeling completely hemmed in by trams and enemy cars, the handsome policeman came down from his throne and charged up to me like a lion, pretending he wanted to eat me. I was unable to run away.

The policeman grabbed me by my arm. His mouth

was huge and open. I really did believe he was a lion; panting cars surrounded me, the traffic lights glowed like red and green eyes, the houses were so high, the sky was remote, clouds of fog whooshed down on top of me. And because the policeman was a lion, I treated him like one. I patted the hand with which he was holding my arm, I implored him in French not to hurt me, and not to hold me so tight and not to eat me if he wasn't hungry, because: *'Mon père n'est pas chez nous et ma mère ne peut pas rester sans moi. Excusez-moi, monsieur. Je vous ai regardé – vous êtes si beau.'*

At that the lion stopped his growling, and he didn't want to arrest me either; the policeman turned into a prince who carried me across the road to the woman who sits on the rails. The woman is fat, and she sells nuts from two big wicker baskets. The trams don't use those rails any more.

The prince set me down in front of the fat woman. I managed to kiss him quickly first. He bought me ten large walnuts from the woman. Then he went away, remounted his throne, and mastered the traffic again. He was just exactly as he had been before, when I felt I had to stare at him, and so brought the traffic to a halt.

Now I see him every day. I always sort of wave to him with my eyes, and he smiles down at me. Sometimes I badly want to wave to him with my hand. But I decide I'd better not. Perhaps it would bring the traffic to a halt.

*

We pass the Rotisserie d'Ardennoise, where we sometimes went with my father. He would drink some pink
wine, or some dark brown beer out of a little silver
goblet. Even if you go in there at lunchtime, it's evening
inside, and there are little yellow lamps burning on the
wooden tables. Once when I knocked over one of those
lamps by accident, it was positively night time at the
table, though the street outside was still perfectly bright.
Now there's a giant beast lying outside the rotisserie,
with a skin like the ground in a pine forest, all black and
needly and rough. There's blood coming out of its head.

My mother pulls me away from it and says: 'That's a
wild boar.' Do those really exist? Where do they live? My
mother says: well, she's never seen one before either, but
she's sure they do, and that's what it is. This one is dead,
and people are going to eat it.

Outside another store there are bundles of large
colourful birds. They once really existed as well; they
flew around somewhere. I would be scared if those birds
were still alive and came flying at me. But the birds are
as dead as the boar, and they're going to be eaten later
as well. Only not with their feathers on. I should like to
know why people won't eat the pretty feathers and what
happens to them, because surely they're the major part
of a bird. Maybe there are factories that are able to convert the feathers into canned vegetables or something?

My mother says: 'Sometimes people stuff pillows with
feathers like that.'

That makes me really keen to cut open our pillows, to check whether they're full of such pretty feathers – and then I'd let the feathers fly out of the window.

The lady with the bird's nest comes out of the big Café Monopole. I want to drag my mother out of the way quickly, but she's already spotted us. I'm a little afraid of the lady with the bird's nest, because she wants to adopt me.

'Maestro' – she has always addressed my father as 'Maestro' – 'Maestro, do you not worry what this nomadic existence is going to do to your daughter? Let me have her, and I'll take that wild bud and develop it into a beautiful blossom of a girl.' But I don't want to be developed by the bird's nest.

We go back inside the Monopole with the bird's nest. I would prefer to sit outside myself, but the bird's nest is afraid of draughts. My mother doesn't want to order anything, because we don't have any money – but the bird's nest does. So I quite simply order a couple of frankfurters for her and a vanilla ice cream for me, and I say very quickly: 'Thank you so much for treating us, Fräulein Brouwer. Next time, when my father's here, we'll treat you.'

'What news of the maestro?' asks Fräulein Brouwer, and then she says: 'Ah, such a creative temperament needs space, no family bonds can be permitted to trammel it.'

We met Fräulein Brouwer on the Moselle once, she was staying at the same hotel as us. She pursued my father, because she knew his books. There isn't a single woman in the whole world to whom my father isn't charming. That's why we often have women buzzing around us that my mother and me aren't able to shoo away by ourselves; my father just attracts them. Fräulein Brouwer is short and old. She used to be a schoolteacher, and now she has a legacy and open eyes and ears and she wants to take in the beauties of the world. That's why she keeps going to places where my father is. My mother hates that sort of behaviour. Once she said to my father: 'The hysterical flattery of women like that is only going to make you even more spoilt than you are already.'

Fräulein Brouwer always addresses my father as '*maître et cher collègue*' too, because when she was staying on the Moselle, she wrote a poem about a bird's nest, which got published in a newspaper. Fräulein Brouwer says she is busy planning her future oeuvre, and that her family have always had a poetic streak.

She is half German and half Dutch, but her passport is Dutch, which is very lucky for her. My father says it used to be important to have a good name or a good reputation, but that no longer matters – what is important is having a good nationality. And that's just what we don't have, and the bird's nest does. If she were to adopt me, I'd have it too, but I'd rather have my mother.

I don't like it when the bird's nest says to me: 'Well, Kully, how is everything?' and acts as though she's terrifically pally with me. I can tell her I've got different pals than her. Nor do I want to be brought up by the bird's nest. Frankly, I'd rather be naughty, and that way she won't want to have me any more.

When we return to the hotel, the hotel manager goes up to my mother in the lobby and says: 'Madame, we have just received a telegram from your husband in Warsaw. He will settle the bill from there in the next few days.'

I'm so happy, but my mother is hardly able to smile. 'From Warsaw?' she says quietly. 'From Warsaw . . .'

In the afternoon, my mother arranges a rendezvous with Herr Fiedler, because she thinks he may know what my father is doing in Warsaw. She's also desperate to talk to a grown-up writer again, and borrow some money so that we can go and have something to eat again.

My mother is always out to borrow money, but when push comes to shove, she doesn't do it. I can understand that stealing from people is wrong, but I fail to understand why one shouldn't ask people for money if they have got some. It annoys me when people don't hand over their money when they have it and we need it. Why do they suppose we go to the trouble of asking? When my father has money, he always gives it to other people who need it.

It's wrong to abandon children and animals, or neglect them, but money isn't something that becomes unhappy or that starts crying if you leave it. My grandmother in Cologne was someone else who always gave money to us, and to other people too. She can't send us any money now, though, because if she did the German government would lock her up.

My mother says my father can't settle the hotel bill from Warsaw anyway, because the Polish government doesn't allow you to send money out of Poland. My father often tells fibs to get a bit of peace and quiet. We're happy about that. Sometimes, though, he performs miracles and everything he says comes true.

My mother is crimping her hair in front of the mirror; she wants to have a round curl either side of her face, to make her look beautiful. If she looks beautiful, she feels better about walking through the lobby or talking to people to ask them for money. I'm not like that when I'm asking for money: I don't mind not looking beautiful.

I watch my mother test her curling tongs on some newspaper beforehand, to make sure they're not too hot. She's just making a face go curly in the newspaper, and I exclaim: 'Look, Mama, there's Uncle Pius!' It's a newspaper from Switzerland that Herr Fiedler gave us last week, after he'd read it. I don't like to read newspapers, and my mother doesn't either. Only sometimes, when I'm not able to sleep. It really is: the newspaper has a big picture of Uncle Pius. My mother looks at it as well, and then her hands shake, and she drops her curling tongs. Under the picture it says: 'The well-known Viennese doctor recently passed away in Vienna; there were no suspicious circumstances.'

'What did Uncle Pius do, Mama?'

'Oh, Kully, don't ask – you won't understand, it's a dreadful world.'

I'm very fond of Uncle Pius. He is our favourite uncle; he's already old and grey-haired. A year ago we stayed with him in Vienna, and we all felt very happy. Uncle Pius laughed a lot, and he was very good to us. Now we can't go back to see Uncle Pius or Vienna, because the German government has occupied it all.

We know lots of people who ran away from Vienna, including even some children. The silly thing is that when you run away from those countries, you have to go as you are, you can't take your house or your money with you. That's the reason why my grandmother stayed in Cologne. Uncle Pius has a big hospital in Vienna – how is he going to take that with him?

My father says the German government locked people up who didn't even steal anything. Who would want to live in a country like that?

'Uncle Pius is dead,' says my mother. 'Just a minute, I'll be right back.' She's crying, and she runs off with the newspaper tucked under her arm. She has given herself a round curl only on one side of her face.

It is very quiet in the room. I pick up the curling tongs and blow out the little blue spirit flame. I wonder why Uncle Pius's death makes my mother cry? My father has said many times: 'The dead are happy. Nothing can happen to them any more.'

If Uncle Pius has died, then he'll be happy and can float around me. Maybe the reason my mother's crying is because she can't ever see him again now. But there are lots of living people we can't see too, because they live in countries with those sorts of governments, or because of the borders, or because they've been locked up.

I have a friend in Frankfurt who's older than me but who still used to play with me. We used to go and ride on our scooters down the Bockenheimer Landstrasse. Once we were in a meadow where there were lots of big rocks. We managed to move some of them by combining all our strength. Underneath the rocks were various little insects and pale-looking grass. We sat there perfectly still and didn't touch anything. We felt like big giants or knights who had liberated whole worlds.

Once a man came along and said to me: 'What are you doing playing with Jewboy?' Then we both felt terribly afraid and ran off together, even though we hadn't done anything wrong.

In the palm house once we ran away from one of the wardens, but that time it was because we had picked some azaleas. That was prohibited, as we knew perfectly well. But this time we hadn't done anything that was prohibited. That's why I told my father all about it that evening. At first he ground his teeth together, and then

he said: 'We're not staying here much longer, Kully –
you can play with anyone you like.'

I wrote letters to my friend, and he wrote letters back.
But then my father said: it's not good for people in
Germany if we write letters to them, and I wasn't to do
it any more. And after that I didn't do it any more. When
it was time for us to leave, I sat and wept with him and
his mother. We won't be able to see each other again.
All we can do is die and then float around one another.

I want to play with my little grocery store, but sometimes
it's no fun on my own. Plus all I have to sell is a couple
of grains of rice and some used matches. It's so horribly
grey in my room; even if I turn on the light it doesn't
seem to get any brighter. I'm not allowed to play near
the window in case I fall out – I promised my mother
that. Otherwise I could watch the trams going by outside,
and the bright fiery sparks they make on the rails. Usually
my mother takes me with her wherever she goes. But
today she left me on my own. Perhaps she won't come
back.

If I cut open our pillows, I could see if they're full of
colourful feathers or not. But I mustn't do anything like
that. My doll's kitchen isn't any fun any more. I can't
cook in it properly with real fire and so on. My mother
said: 'Now, Kully, when we have our own stove again,
or our own room with a spirit cooker, then I'll teach you
how to light a fire and how to cook.' But I know how to

light a fire already. It's not at all hard; all you need is a box of matches and something flammable.

My mother told me I was to wait for her. But I might still pop over to see Madame Rostand anyway. I like her a lot, only she lives a long way away, and I might get lost, and then my mother would have to cry even more. Madame Rostand is my piano teacher and my French teacher. That is, I know how to speak French, of course; Madame Rostand just teaches me how to write it.

Madame Rostand is small and gaudy. Her face is gaudy, and her dress is gaudy. She talks terriblyquickly and she moves terriblyquickly and she laughs terriblyquickly. I wonder what it would be like to play spinning tops with Madame Rostand. If I were the size of a big house, then Madame Rostand would be my little tiny spinning top.

I used to have some lovely spinning tops that I would play with with my friend in Frankfurt. We would make them dance and skip over the ground. We had to whip them so that they would jump and dance over the smooth paving stones and never get tired and fall over.

Madame Rostand is married to an old waiter in our hotel, who is a friend of my father's. Sometimes my mother and I go to call on her of an afternoon. Then she shows me how to write in French, and I play around on her piano, and we laugh together. She once said to my mother: '*Oh, ma petite, ma chère petite, ma belle petite – il ne faut jamais pleurer. Qu'est-ce que c'est – un homme? Il faut rire, ma petite.*'

43

And she went on to say: 'A good husband always has a bad wife – and a bad husband always has a good wife. It has to be that way. I think it's better to be a good wife and to have a bad husband, because a good husband won't make you happy either, but at least with a bad husband you won't be bored.'

My mother couldn't understand that, so I had to translate it. Then I said: 'But my father's not a bad man.'

Then Madame Rostand laughed and said: 'No, he's a good man – only bad husbands are good men. Monsieur is lighthearted and charming; it's only such men who can be loving and faithful. There are husbands who are faithful because they don't love any woman, not even their own wife. I, Madame, prefer a man who is capable of loving and of being loved – even if I'm not the only woman he loves.'

The room has become very quiet. The air outside is thick and woolly. It would be nice if it snowed here like it snowed in Poland. Perhaps my father went to Poland because he wanted to see snow again. Snow is a lovely thing.

My tortoises are rubbing at the wallpaper; I think maybe they're hungry. Wallpaper isn't edible, not even for tortoises. I'm going to go down to the hotel kitchen and ask for some food for my pets.

In the hotel kitchen it's always steamy and frantic. I get in lots of people's way. The day before yesterday a waiter tripped over me with some mulled wine, but no one was hurt. A cook threatened to put me in a saucepan if I ever went down there again. But the others quickly gave me some things for my tortoises to eat, to be rid of me.

I don't think it's allowed to cook people – the cook won't really do anything like that. But the cauldrons in the kitchen are so big, and once I got into a bathtub where the water was very hot. That was terribly painful. I'm not frightened to go to the kitchen, but my father once said: 'Nowadays any sort of atrocity is possible.'

I'm in the room again, my mother isn't back yet. I haven't been boiled and I have some food for my tortoises. It is a difficult and dangerous thing, looking after one's animals.

I sit in front of my grocer's shop; I can't be tired because I can feel my heart pounding. Why do I have my grocer's shop if I don't even have enough to feed my tortoises? I plonk them down at my side. The lady with the bird's nest asked me once: 'What are they called?'

I said: 'Tortoises.'

'Didn't you give them a name, Kully?'

'They've got a name, they're called tortoises.'

'Do you give them numbers then, Kully? Are they Tortoise One and Two?'

'No, they're both tortoises.'

The lady with the bird's nest just wouldn't understand. She said: 'You haven't inherited your father's imagination, you lack that wonderful childish imagination. When I was a girl I called my canaries Johannes and Charlotte.'ffi,

'Why should my tortoises be called Johannes and Charlotte?'

Then she said: 'But surely you have to call them sometimes, and talk to them. How do you address them then?'

I didn't say anything after that, there's no point in talking to people as stupid as that. Tortoises aren't dogs, for Lord's sake, that you can call; they can't hear. Tortoises need food, and in return they stay alive, crawl around and rub at the wallpaper when I'm alone with them in a room.

'Dearest Annie –' I didn't want to open the letter, but then I did anyway because it was an express letter. The bellboy brought it up to the room. I laid the letter on the table and kept staring at it. Express letters always look so excited and can't bear not to be opened right away. You're not supposed to open other people's letters, though; my mother wouldn't like it. The letter is from my father. I always recognize his writing.

I tried to wait for my mother; she didn't come. I waited for her and I counted up to thirty – when she still wasn't there, I opened the letter. I think it's better than getting

* Probably do-goodishly inspired by J. W. von Goethe and Charlotte von Stein. (Trans.)

silly ideas. The lady with the bird's nest says: 'Unoccupied children are always apt to have silly ideas.'

'Dearest Annie,' writes my father:

Dearest Annie,

I am so worried about you both. How are you, how is Kully? Send me a wire right away, to set my mind at rest. I won't be able to work until I hear from you. And I really need to work. I've heard nothing from you for weeks.

I couldn't let you have an address for me; I didn't have one. Wherever I ended up, I had to leave or wanted to leave right away. In Prague I couldn't do any deals, beyond selling a couple of newspaper articles. And you know what sort of money the Prague papers pay.

By chance I ran into an old acquaintance. He has a theatre publishing firm in Switzerland now and is looking for plays. I spent an evening with him, and had a marvellous idea for a comedy. Allowed myself to be talked into writing it by my friend. The advance paid for me to get as far as Budapest. I must deliver a script in eight weeks. It would be pretty shoddy of me if I didn't, he's really a decent fellow. Never written a comedy before, mind, and I've forgotten what my idea was. But I'll think of something.

In Budapest, I was paid some money by my Hungarian publishers, the Giganten-Verlag. Of course they should have paid me ages ago, and of course they pleaded the restrictions on exporting currency.

I feel rotten and ill. I don't know what to do. I miss you

horribly, and must talk to you. I hate writing letters – a bigger strain than writing three chapters of a novel. You're going to have to grit your teeth and fend for yourself, Annie, till we're back together.

In Budapest, I got a letter from Genek, who invites us. Manya wants a divorce from him finally. But he can't stand to be on his own. A business associate of his gave me money for the fare to Warsaw. I'd got everything I could out of the Budapest publishers. By the end, those people were as tough as granite.

By the way, I sent you and Kully a Hungarian national costume apiece on your birthdays. I'm sure you must look charming in them. My Hungarian translator got hold of them for me. She has the most beautiful small hands, and her life is hard, believe me. It's rare for small hands to be beautiful. Either they're like sad little bundles of bones – chilly skeleton hands – or else they're silly pink pudgy pillows. Oh Christ, Annie. See, I'm starting to address an epistolary novel to you. A sure sign of my disintegration. A novelist shouldn't go all literary in his letters.

From Warsaw I travelled to Lvov with Genek. Here I'm staying at the Hotel Europejski. Genek's affection for me has cooled somewhat since paying my last hotel bill. I appealed to his sense of family, even though I have really not the least idea whether he and I are actually related. He now expects me seriously to live in his horrible house, surrounded by more old mothers and aunts and sisters than ever, interspersed with small children – I never manage to learn whose.

The entire household boasts just two liqueur glasses, neither of them larger than a hazelnut, and one bottle of home-distilled pear brandy, which is expected to furnish several more generations. And every day I have to spend hours there! Genek and the rest of them treat me like the Salvation Army treats a fallen woman. Kamelia of her kindness gave me a glass of raspberry syrup with lemon in it, which I promptly puked up in the bath.

And they're not proud of me any more either, the way they were last year. Seeing my picture in the papers, and my books in the windows of bookshops, doesn't impress them at all any more. To his intimates, a famous writer with no money is like an old con artist. He's like a duke with no castle and no servants.

Last year they seemed to see the fame more than the poverty. Our poverty had something theatrical for them, the poverty of a young millionaire, forced by his wise father to make the discovery (over a week or two) that life is a serious business. Now they understand that my penury is permanent and genuine. People don't like to be disappointed like that. As a result, what I get from them is no longer hospitality but charity. My God, what can one expect from a family that trades in non-ferrous metals? People like that are incorrigible romantics, with imaginations like quick-drying cement. An unknown poet belongs in a garret, a famous one in a castle in Hollywood.

Genek's cousin Rosi, who looks sour and greenish and is interested in literature, has borrowed books of mine from the lending library three times in succession now. It's her way of supporting me, and she now gads about like a benefactress.

The day before yesterday Kamelia took me up to a windy promontory in Stilitzky Park. There I was to sit down on a bench and write an ode to the beautiful view. She is one of those people who are incapable of seeing a writer without pressing pencil and paper upon him, and sticking him in a rose-grown gazebo or a belvedere or a bench in a leafy forest glade. Normally such creatures are at their deadliest in spring and summer. Kamelia, I'm sorry to say, has the condition so badly that she is oblivious to the weather. She wanders around, seeking out benches for me. The fresh air is supposed to be intellectually stimulating, head-clearing and health-bringing all at the same time. I have had to tell her I am not a *plein air* poet! Since then, I'm afraid she's lost her faith in me.

That's a pity, because I think she has some influence over Genek in money matters; she helps him with the non-ferrous metals, and is staggeringly efficient in such matters as share ownership and foreign bank accounts. With business partners she is deft and sure-footed. She wouldn't dream of telling such a man to sit down on a damp park bench with the instruction to stay there till the cool evening breeze blew along with it the tintinnabulations of the local church.

Genek also requires that I eat lunch at their house. When lunch is over, the family drives me out on to the balcony to order me to take deep breaths. And after that I am to take a nap. So concerned are they that I lead a healthy life that I feel I'm going to hell in a handcart.

Annie, it's really high time something were done. I have got Genek to the point where he will transfer travelling funds for you and Kully from his London account. He thinks we will then all move in with him. Kamelia is very keen to give Kully lessons. I no longer impress this branch of my family, but they don't yet want to be shot of me – they want to save me. Of course I won't hear of you coming. You should use the travelling money for Poland to pay the hotel bill, and then go to Amsterdam with Kully. Once you're there, nothing can happen to you. Go to the Palace Hotel; it's expensive but at least the manager owes me sixty guilders. It's a start. The man's name is Flens, and he's a very good friend of mine – you can trust him.

Once in Amsterdam, head straight to my publishers. You must tell Krabbe that you've got the completed manuscript of the new novel in your possession. Of course you won't be able to give it to him, as it doesn't exist. But you must do all in your power to make him think it's finished. When I'm back in Amsterdam, I'll knock off the last two hundred pages in a week. I'll work day and night. As you know, Annie, I've worked a lot harder than that. Somehow, things have always panned out so far.

Krabbe won't give much for your literary views, so you have to tell him this new novel is a real page-turner. Let him think he'll have a popular success on his hands. You have to get Krabbe so primed that he'll wire me some travel money.

He used to be a nice tender-hearted fellow, a man who was capable of warm feeling and friendship. Unfortunately, his character has recently suffered a change for the worse. I remember a time when I could get advances out of him by the simple expedient of writing letters. And today? If you read my epistolary cries for help to the moon, it would fall weeping from the heavens. But Krabbe is as tough as old boots. Of course times are hard – not least for a publisher bringing out German-language books abroad – but Krabbe takes things too far.

Take Kully with you when you go to Krabbe's office. Don't write to let him know you're coming; don't even let his secretary announce you, in case he runs away. I can't believe he will be as inhuman when confronted with women and children. Kully should put on her white dress that she looks so sweet in. Don't leave before he's wired me the money. Chain yourselves to his desk, if necessary.

Now pull yourself together, Annie. Do everything right – I'm relying on you. Before long we'll be back together! Then we'll go to Paris. France is a marvellous country, nowhere is as cheap.

Have you kept our three tickets for the Belgian Colonial Lottery? They'll be making the prize draw in the next few days. For God's sake, get a copy of the list of winners in good time. I'm sorry, but sometimes you're a bit absent-minded in these business affairs, and I really have to think of everything. The numbers gave me a good feeling. Maybe we'll be lucky this time.

Please don't forget to telephone Popp once before you leave Brussels. In Ostende I gave him some really wonderful advertising concepts for his department stores. It might be that Popp has already been successful with one or other of them? My head is so full I can't follow through on everything myself, and it's easily possible that we thereby might miss out on some huge sums. Perhaps you can get Popp to give you an advance on some of the ideas. But that won't be easy. It takes incredible virtuosity to separate someone like Popp from even a little bit of his money.

I've written a postcard to Fräulein Brouwer – remember, the one with the bird's nest? In case the Polish travel money isn't enough to get you to Amsterdam, let her help you out. In return, I'll cut her into the royalties for my comedy.

I must go now. Manya's just come to collect me. She says to say hello to you, she's as charming as ever. I don't know whether I really should tell her to stay with Genek, in that muddle of old and ageing women, none of whom like her, never mind understand her.

Goodbye, my dears! Kisses!

We're now in Amsterdam, our third day already. When we arrived, the city was decked out in orange flags, but not for us.fflw My mother and I are sitting in a restaurant

---

* Orange is the national colour of the Netherlands because its royal family used to own the principality of Orange. The celebrations were, most likely, for the fortieth anniversary of Queen Wilhelmina in 1938. (Trans.)

near the railway station, which floats on the black water. The sun is shining, ships sail by, motorboats moor at our feet.

We are waiting for Herr Krabbe. Maybe he'll let me have a ride in a motorboat. He can be very nice sometimes, but at other times he gives me such a scowl, it's as though he wishes I didn't exist. Yesterday he refused to go and feed the gulls with me.

I can't speak to my mother. She is wearing a frown of concentration. Probably she's thinking about how to explain to Herr Krabbe that she's forgotten to bring my father's manuscript again.

I am writing a postcard to Madame Rostand. She doesn't know Amsterdam at all, or France either. But my father once told her that she was a special type of Belgian woman who was more French than the French.

Amsterdam is very beautiful. It is made up of rivers which are called *grachten*. You're not allowed to swim in them, because they're poisonous. The flowers here are even lovelier than elsewhere. Because of the monarchy, a lot of them are yellow.

The hotel we're staying in is so lovely and distinguished that we forget to breathe when we walk across the lobby. My mother thinks we don't even look like guests any more, more like women bringing sheets and towels for the guests, or come to collect clothes for laundering and ironing. In the summer we were beautiful and could walk around in sandals and sheer dresses, but what about now?

Maybe my grandmother will come from Germany to see us, and bring some warm clothes and coats with her. But my mother doesn't want to write and tell her all the things we need, in case she holds it against my father.

It's cold here beside the water. We laid our heavy travelling plaids round our shoulders. But my mother doesn't want to be seen going in and out of the hotel wrapped in blankets like that.

Last night in the hotel room we put on the lovely cheerful Hungarian folk costumes my father sent us. When the chambermaid came in to turn back the sheets, she asked us if we didn't have a flyer or a playbill, because she was so sure we belonged to some travelling dance troupe.

Herr Krabbe called to say he was waiting for us downstairs in the café. I ran down as quickly as I could. Because it happens to be a fact that Herr Krabbe always gets a free dish of nuts from the waiters, but in return he has to drink some really horrible drink called Bols. If I so much as sniff it, it makes me splutter. My father always drinks medicine like that. Herr Krabbe lets me take his nuts.

All the people in the café except Herr Krabbe have looked at me and complimented me on my beautiful national costume. He thought it was about time my mother came down, but she has to get changed first. Imagine if she came down in the Hungarian national costume!

Herr Krabbe asked me about the manuscript for the novel. I said: 'It's in a suitcase.'

'Will your mother be bringing it downstairs with her?' asked Herr Krabbe, looking at me with squinting eyes.

'I don't know, Herr Krabbe.'

Herr Krabbe wants the novel, but my mother and I don't have a manuscript. What to do?

'Do lots of people write novels, Herr Krabbe?'

'What do you mean "lots"? Everyone writes novels.'

'My mother isn't writing a novel.'

'Really? You surprise me.'

'Is the waiter here writing a novel?'

'Bound to be.'

'Does everyone have to write a novel?'

'No.'

'Why does my father have to, then?'

'Because he knows how it's done.'

'Do the other people not know how it's done, then?'

'Almost never.'

'So why do they write novels?'

'Because they don't know they can't.'

'Can children write novels, Herr Krabbe?'

'No. Even though people who set themselves to write novels are children.'

'My father isn't a child.'

'Oh yes, he is.'

'But that can't be true. My father's as tall as you.'

'Taller.'

'Herr Krabbe, is it really true that no child has ever written a novel?'

'Yes.'

'Do you think a well-behaved child could if she tried hard and applied herself?'

'No.'

'Not even if she practises on the typewriter?'

'No – oh, for God's sake, don't cry – what's your name again? Kully? Here, eat some nuts, drink some more orangeade, be brave. What would you say to some ice cream? Your dress is really very pretty. You've turned into such a big girl, I can't sit you on my lap any more. When will your mother come? I want to go to bed. You can't yet write a novel for your father – he'll have to do it all by himself, and maybe he really will deliver it soon.'

'I'm sure he will, Herr Krabbe. He only needs another two hundred pages.'

'Oh, my God,' said Herr Krabbe.

My mother walked in. Herr Krabbe struggled to get out of his chair, kissed her hand, and said: 'As a publisher I'd like to be Pope, and enforce celibacy on all my authors.'

'Why?' said my mother, and: 'Oh God, now I've gone and left the manuscript upstairs – I'll give it to you tomorrow, Herr Krabbe.'

I was sent to bed, but I didn't want to go to sleep. Why shouldn't a child write a novel? If an angel could perform a miracle and I could straight away type out two hundred pages of a novel, then we'd be saved.

When my mother and me arrived in Amsterdam two days ago, the first thing we did was sleep. Then my mother put me into the white dress, and we went to Herr Krabbe's office. In the history book my mother is teaching me from, there is a picture of a veiled Queen Louise, standing imploringly before a grim and dark Napoleon.

That's how my mother stood before Herr Krabbe as she asked him to send money to my father. Herr Krabbe was holding in his hand a telegram from my father that said: 'Beg your protection for helpless wife and child.' That meant Mama and me.

Herr Krabbe lifted both hands to his head, and squashed it between them. He showed my mother books full of sums, and each sum a line and a total. He said my father should have delivered his new novel to them six months ago already. He had kept on promising the completed manuscript, and already drawn an awful lot of money on it in the form of advances.

My mother said: 'The novel's finished. I've got it in the hotel room.'

Herr Krabbe sent my father the travel money he

needed. That was our first visit to Herr Krabbe; since then we've seen quite a bit of him.

Now we're sitting by the waterside, waiting for him again. Maybe he'll turn up on his bicycle, and then I can try to ride it. Everyone here goes around on bicycles all the time, and they're a lot of very happy cyclists. Only Herr Krabbe is an earnest-looking cyclist; he never hums or whistles to himself as he rides. Nor does he ride no-hands either. I only hope my father will be back soon.

We're in a great state of alarm about the hotel now. If only we could move out! My mother doesn't dare ask what the room is costing us. We are staying in the same hotel as a bunch of Maharajas – those are the richest men in the world.

My father wanted us to talk to the manager, Herr Flens, right away, about the sixty guilders he owed my father. But it was very disagreeable for my mother to go and talk about that with Herr Flens right away. So, because we didn't even have the money for the tram to go to Herr Krabbe, she just sat quietly in our room for a couple of hours, to overcome her embarrassment. When she had overcome enough of it, she went downstairs with me, and asked for Herr Flens. He came out right away, short and fat, with Chinese eyes. He was very pleased to learn that we were associated with my father, and that my father sent him a greeting. And he said he had long wanted to have an address for my father, who still owed him sixty guilders. The money would certainly come in handy now.

My father must have got everything mixed up. My mother said it was terribly difficult to be married to my father. I asked my mother whether she would like it better to be married to the Maharajas, and she replied: 'No, not that either.'

I would really like to be married to the Maharajas. They are so lovely and brown, naturally brown, even in the middle of winter. To get like that, other people have to lie down in the burning sun for months.

Next to our hotel stands a man with a big cart, with lots and lots of jars of herrings and gherkins on it. I am friends with the man, but the only way I can speak to him is if I pinch my nose shut, because the herrings smell so. The man speaks Dutch, but even so I can almost always understand what he says. He has a face like a scrunched-up piece of paper, blue eyes and blond hair. His father is dead, but he still has a mother, and two sisters and no children, and no wife either, because he can't afford one. He loves his herrings and his onions and his mother – he didn't mention his sisters.

He told me some more about the Maharajas. I'm pretty certain I'm going to marry a Maharaja now. The Maharajas will give me a diamond as big as an egg. Once I have a diamond like that, I'll be able to buy all the hotels in the world, and my parents and I will be able to travel fearlessly from hotel to hotel. We will never have to pay a bill, and we will always be able to leave just exactly when we feel like it.

It seems a Maharaja has several wives, which I think is a good thing. That way when he has to leave, I won't be alone but will be able to turn to the other wives for comfort. I don't know whether it's allowed to marry several Maharajas. Obviously that would be the best. Then, if a couple of them had to travel to Poland, I'd still have a few more to hand. My mother is a great example of how difficult it is for a woman who has to get by on just one man.

At last Herr Krabbe has turned up in our restaurant by the waterside. He looks dark and angry, like a cannibal. It seems more writers have turned up in Amsterdam, so Herr Krabbe really has his hands full, because they're all after him for money.

Herr Krabbe has a letter from my father, who says the travel money he sent wasn't enough, and he's to send more, and also that it was inhuman on the part of Krabbe to keep a man away from his wife and child; in addition he had a pitiable creature whom he had to comfort over in Poland. That pitiable creature is Manya.

Herr Krabbe says he thinks it's perfectly possible that my father might marry a second wife somewhere else out of pure absent-minded politeness. He wanted my mother to write and inform him that Herr Krabbe would not consider himself responsible for any further families of my father's, and would not support him either if he should find himself locked up for bigamy.

Bigamy is the thing the Maharajas do, but they're allowed to. My father is only allowed to have my mother and me. My mother approves of that arrangement too.

Mama is crying. Herr Krabbe has had it up to here with misery. He even forgets to ask after the manuscript; instead he orders milk, cake and coffee for us.

My mother has no use for Manya, but my father does. When we were in Poland a year ago, he kept on comforting her. Manya is as beautiful as a princess in the fairytale books my mother reads to me. In the cafés in Poland, I always wanted to hold my cold hands in front of Manya's eyes, to make them warm. Those are the sort of eyes Manya has.

Manya is the wife of Uncle Genek. I suppose she's my aunt really. But she's not a real aunt. Real aunts don't sparkle like that, and they aren't so nice-smelling either. Uncle Genek isn't a real uncle either. He has terribly big ears, and in the middle of them he looks very small and sad. He walks much too fast – a real uncle has a different sort of walk.

We met Uncle Genek last year in Vienna; that's when my father discovered that they were related. Uncle Genek invited us to visit them in Poland. We really don't mind where we go, so long as it's inside some country or other.

My father was able to give a series of lectures in Poland too, but I wasn't allowed to listen. The thing about lectures is that they always take place after bedtime. I so badly wanted to go, because thousands of lights are turned on in wonderful castles, and lots of people come, all beautiful and sparkling like the evening star. I imagine a lecture must be something like thunder made out of diamonds.

Cars came to collect my father. My mother calmed me down and said all that was going to happen was that my father was going to speak. After that I could fall asleep quite easily, because I know what it's like when my father speaks. Only: why is speaking sometimes called 'lecture', and sometimes just 'speaking'?

When we arrived in Poland, Manya and Uncle Genek were living in Lvov in a large cold dark house where lots of aunt-like women eddied back and forth. My father declined to live there with them. Then I was supposed to live there, but my mother didn't want that. My father has got lots of people, but my mother has only me.

We moved into a small hotel. There were seventeen men in navy caps waiting outside the door, merely in order to open the door for the guests – that was probably their livelihood. Our room was as bright as summer, but when we looked out of the window, we saw a world that was all Christmas.

I asked my mother if that was really all snow. She said: 'Yes.'

I could hardly believe it. The snow came down from

the sky. The whole of the earth was white with snow, glistening. Stars shone down on the houses, pine trees stood in the big square, and in the very middle of it stood the Almighty, watching over everything like a big dark pillar. My father, though, said it wasn't the Almighty at all, but some Polish general. That may have been the case during the day, at night it was certainly the Almighty.

The whole of the earth was white – I felt so glad. Sleighs drove by carrying Christmas manger straw, and other sleighs hailed them by ringing their bells. I secretly ran down very fast and jumped into the snow.

Sometimes the snow got to be very slippery-smooth. Once, my mother fell down in the middle of Akademizki. Then a whole regiment of marching soldiers picked her up. After that we bought galoshes for her. But she kept on taking timid little steps, just like the aunts when they left that big dark house.

They don't have taxis in Lvov. We only ever saw one, and that was broken. So we always took a sleigh when we went to the Café Roma at lunchtime. There, all the men kissed my mother's hand and complimented her. My father assembled crowds around him at table. Everyone drank green schnapps, as green as the traffic lights in Brussels and Amsterdam. The men wore black cloth blinkers over their ears and noses, because the cold ate away human extremities. It's my belief that only the men suffer in this way, because the women never went around with black blinkers on their faces, nor did I ever see one without a nose or ears.

My mother wasn't able to pronounce Polish very well, so I had to learn it for her. I made friends with the daughter of the toilet lady in the Roma, and with a man who stood near the hotel, and sold lighters on the sly. If you must know, the Polish government is against lighters. I sometimes helped the man whisper into people's ears, and if they didn't buy anything, we swore at them together.

In a new country the first words I learn are ones my father thinks are indecent, and I'm not meant to say them. But it's a pity to have to give up any of the very few words at your disposal. And when I've said them, people have always looked at me extra fondly.

Just now in Amsterdam Herr Krabbe told me not to say a certain indecent Dutch word, so I decided I had better talk to him.

'Herr Krabbe, is my spit decent so long as it's in my mouth?'

'Yes.'

'Herr Krabbe, is my spit indecent if I spit it on the table here?'

'Yes. Your spit is, and you are.'

'Herr Krabbe, is it indecent if I say "spit"?'

'"Saliva" might be considered better.'

'Is saliva the same as spit?'

'Yes.'

'Herr Krabbe, if I spit my saliva on the table, is that still indecent?'

'Yes.'

'Herr Krabbe, if my saliva on the table is indecent and the word "saliva" is decent, what makes a word indecent?'

'Goddamnit, I've had enough of this. I don't care – you can use all the bad language you like.'

'Herr Krabbe, why is saliva that I've spat out indecent anyway?'

'It's not indecent at all, it's you who are indecent. Spit doesn't belong on the table, because it makes it dirty. Anyway spitting is disgusting.'

'Herr Krabbe, if I spit spit I'm indecent, but if I say "spit" I'm not indecent, because surely it's just a word?'

'Oh, child! Just a word! What do you know about words!'

'I know lots of bad words, Herr Krabbe.'

When we were in Poland, we ate lots of red soup and white chicken, and sometimes I was allowed to drink sweet molten honey, which is called mead. When I'd had some of that, I was as happy as a cloud.

Akademizki is a street, a wide street with black bare trees either side of it, and people running up and down it. My mother calls streets like that 'promenade'. There were men on it who wore fur caps. And sometimes men rushed past who had had their faces all wrapped up in beards and hair, not because it was cold, but so that they could be Jewish and pleasing unto the Lord.

That's what Uncle Genek told me. I'm not sure if it's true. Sometimes people don't tell me the truth. I believed that it was pleasing unto the Lord if people wore a lot of hair. And now I knew also why my father didn't want to be bald, and why Mary Mother of God had lots of hair too.

In the afternoon I had to go into the gloomy house with the gloomy aunts. They asked me about my mother. I said: 'She wants to be pleasing unto the Lord.'

In the evening the gloomy aunts and my father both asked me: 'Why did you lie? You knew your mother wasn't in church, but at the hairdresser's.'

'But she was in church.'

'Kully, did your mother say she was going to church?'

'But the hairdresser always rubs some stuff in her hair to make it grow.'

They didn't understand me at all. I couldn't speak any more, because all of a sudden the words in my head hid themselves. They all thought I was telling lies, or I was ill. A doctor was supposed to come too. My mother was in church, I wasn't lying.

There are always secrets. I have a secret too, because I wanted to use the Polish cold to make raspberry ice and I broke seven glasses in the process. It happened this way: I was allowed raspberry syrup in my room because

I had a temperature. I saved the raspberry syrup, and then I secretly collected glasses from all the hotel rooms that were left unlocked. I was so desperate to make raspberry ice. I filled seven glasses with raspberry syrup and stood the glasses outside on the window ledge because overnight everything turns to ice. By morning, the night had shattered my glasses.

I didn't want to bring it up: people never believe that things are perfectly capable of breaking by themselves, they would all have thought I was fibbing. At least I had some pink ice – you couldn't really eat it, but it was nice to look at. I wanted to sell it and give my father the money for the broken glasses. But then I thought I would try and eat it, though unfortunately it didn't taste as nice as I'd hoped. I held individual pieces up in the sun, like glowing pink diamonds, and they slowly melted. My whole bed felt wet, and I got up and sat in a chair, and stopped feeling ill.

My parents came in with the doctor. I told him right away: 'I've broken seven glasses.' He held my head and looked at me and said: 'She's completely restored, and has no temperature.' My mother threw the broken glasses in the wastepaper basket.

I hope my father isn't cold in Poland. Maybe Uncle Genek will treat him to a coat. Because the thing is our winter coats are in pawn in Salzburg. In Salzburg, I was almost killed by the Duke of Windsor.

When we went to Poland, we still had our coats. And then we went to Salzburg. It was sunny and the air was warm, and the snow on the mountain peaks was far away. We were glad to get to Salzburg. In Lvov there wasn't any more snow, it was all dirty grey slush.

My mother got really annoyed one last time in Lvov. We went with one aunt through the Jewish market, past tin and rusty scrap iron. The whole market was rusty scrap iron, the sky was yellow. And everything was broken. Broken beds, broken prams, broken wheels of prams, broken lamps, broken screws. Everything was rusty, even the people were broken and rusty.

Then we saw my father walking through the rust with Manya. She was carrying some red roses. My father bought six rusty nails and gave three of them to Manya. She laughed, her face glowed pink under her green lacquered cap. My father looked very serious. First he looked at Manya, then he looked at my mother . . .

My mother didn't want my father to give Manya rusty nails; she told him he should throw them away. My father said: 'Rusty nails are lucky.'

I've now got a collection of thirty rusty nails, but they're not bought, I got them off loose toilet doors. I've also got a couple of old bolts for toilet doors – I don't know whether they're worth anything or not.

My mother wanted to get out. My father wanted to get out as well, he always wants to get out. In a breakfast bar he had a lot of nut brandy to drink, which sometimes poisons him. These breakfast bars don't offer breakfast at all, but all kinds of eating goes on in them at noon and night time. A thousand filled rolls filled the bar, which was way too small.

Uncle Genek and the aunts seemed to like us less. The winter was over, everything was over, our visas were over too. We left without any money. Our relations gave us a little brown suitcase. We thanked them heartily.

We had to travel a day and a night to get from Lvov to Salzburg. We were hungry and opened the little brown suitcase. I was so impatient to see what was in it. My throat felt like an endless tube full of hunger.

The night sprinkled starlight into our apartment. I wanted to eat, we all wanted to eat something. But the suitcase had nothing in it but strings of dried mushrooms which we couldn't eat. They didn't even look nice when you hung them round your neck. My mother said quietly: they'll keep, she might be able to make soup from them one day.

We arrived in Salzburg feeling very hungry and tired. We had hoped to be merry. Some men were going to come and give my father money. They wanted to make films out of his books.

I was in a cinema once, and I saw Shirley Temple. That's the name of a little girl who's pretty and poor, but really she's perfectly all right. My father said: 'That kid's worth millions!'

Millions is a lot of money. If you put a coin on the ground and more and more coins on top of it, till the pile has reached the sky – that's a million.

I can jump around and be merry anywhere, I don't need money for that. But it seems grown-ups need money to be merry. They have a far harder time of it than children, if you ask me.

We wanted to sit in the Café Bazaar and see the colourful Englishmen in their Tyrolean hats. There are no Tyroleans in Salzburg, only English. My mother didn't feel like going to the Café Bazaar. She felt like wandering over water meadows by the river, stroking blossoming shrubs, and sitting on a bench.

My mother and I spend a lot of time sitting on benches. We open our mouths to let the sun shine into them; then we eat the sunshine, and our bellies feel full of warm happy life. My father didn't feel like eating sunshine. He wanted to sit in the Café Bazaar and drink slivovitz, which he finds more warming than any amount of sunshine.

We were standing on a bridge, the river looked so jolly. All at once my mother ran off to the white mountaintops, and to a friend of hers who was waiting for her in the Café Glockenspiel.

My father doesn't like glockenspiels of any kind. He went to the Café Bazaar with me. As long as there's a lot of ice on the mountains, there's not much to be had in cafés. Instead I had Linzer torte. My father drank very sweet black coffee and a lot of slivovitz, which smells of plums. We were on the lookout for famous actors and film producers with lots of money. Not one came – only a waiter, who wanted my father to pay the bill.

I had to stay behind and wait. My father went off; he was going to fetch our coats from the hotel and go with a policeman to take them to the pawn shop. I had to sit in the window and look at the pictures in a magazine. It always makes me terribly tired, having to sit quietly alone. Suddenly my eyes just seem to fall asleep.

All at once everything turned completely horrible. Some people knocked over my table and me with it. My face was in the ashes and dirt, and people rushed madly up to the window, squashing me. I had completely stopped moving. I didn't even cry, because I thought I must have been trampled to death. There were so many shoes all round me.

Suddenly all the shoes were gone, the waiter picked up the table and put it back, found me and put me back too. At first I yelled that I didn't want to be put back, because once again people were coming running up to me. They wanted to sit me down on a chair, and touch me. They brought me cake. But I fought back, I kicked and spat, and threw cake at them.

My father came back, I recognized him. 'My God,' he cried, 'what happened?'

I screamed: 'I've been trampled to death.'

He sat me down on his lap. 'Are you injured? Does something hurt?'

'No. I told you: I'm dead. They trampled me to death.'

'But Kully, you're alive, you're moving around. What are you doing with that piece of cake?'

'I want to throw it at the people and kill them in return for trampling me to death.'

I was dead, but my father wouldn't believe me. Tables danced and trees came; I wanted to break them, there was iron in my hands – and then I flew very far away.

Opposite the Café Bazaar is a shop that sells dirndls, and loden coats and loden trousers. That was where the Duke of Windsor went in to buy something. Everyone wanted to see the Duke of Windsor for themselves, and that's what the mass running was about. It was my misfortune to have been sitting directly in the window.

Later on, my father pointed out the Duke to me. He doesn't look like much, if you ask me. I can't understand people knocking over small children just for a sight of him. He used to be a king, apparently, and he really belongs in England.

The policeman was paid from the money that my father got for the coats. There was enough left for us to go to the Augustinerbrau in the evening too, to buy radishes and salt pretzels in the cobbled streets of the monastery and fill big jugs full of beer at the fountain. I didn't drink any, I was only allowed to carry the jugs, and walk around singing in the big hall among the tables.

My mother was cross that my father had taken away the coats. I thought it was silly of my father not to have taken away my coat too, because it was stolen later, at the border in Buchs. And now we can't go back to Salzburg to pick up our coats, because there's a dangerous new regime in power.

That's why my mother and I are in Amsterdam. But we have to leave here too, because the police won't let us stay as our visa stamps are no longer valid. And my father still isn't back. Herr Krabbe did give us some money once, but not enough. We couldn't quite pay for the hotel.

The Dutch queen has a jubilee, and Amsterdam is preparing a carnival for her. The city is fluttering in yellow. Everyone is playing music; a man stood in front of our hotel and ate fire – I saw that with my own eyes.

Christmas is coming soon. What am I going to give my mother? She wants to die sometimes, then she'll have quiet and not be afraid any more. But then she doesn't know what will become of me. I don't want to die yet, because I'm still just a girl. My mother would like to be a chambermaid and work and earn money. But the various countries won't let her be a chambermaid.

The world has grown dark, because of rain and war. Herr Krabbe knows all there is to know about war. War is something that comes and makes everything dead. Then there'll be nowhere left for me to play, and bombs will keep falling on my head.

Herr Krabbe has stopped coming to see us. I rode into

a *gracht* on his bicycle, but only the bicycle went in. There
are no railings on the *grachten*, it's quite easy for that to
happen. It was a particularly lovely *gracht* on Rem-
brandtsplein, beautiful flower barges were floating on it
like gardens in the water.

I'm glad I didn't fall in as well. I once saw a rat
swimming in a *gracht* near the station. The rat was a
witch, and it was after me. On the whole Herr Krabbe
was pleased that his bicycle went in without me, but he
wasn't really pleased.

My mother is in bed, because she's ill. She doesn't want
to sleep with me any more; she wants to lie on the
ground at night so I don't get infected. She still loves me,
though. I'd love to sleep on the ground once in my life;
after all, I spend so much time sitting on it. We have a
grey carpet in our room, and it's as soft as a mown
meadow.

When the telephone rings, my mother has to get up
and go to the other side of the room in her blue nightie.
In Amsterdam, they don't have telephones installed next
to the beds. I asked Herr Flens about it, and he explained.
People often want to be woken in the morning, and so
the telephone rings to wake them. And they shouldn't
just be able to pick up the receiver and stay in bed, they
should have to get up.

Herr Krabbe said the hotels would shortly invent
something that would sprinkle cold water from the

ceiling over their guests. We don't care anyway; we don't need waking, we can sleep all the time.

My mother is lying there, so hot and so quiet. She says: 'We're finished.' I went and sat next to the old liftboy in the pink jacket. We asked ourselves: 'What shall we do?'

My mother didn't want to play anything with me any more. Normally we play all the time. We play: how many beds have you slept in? Or: how many trains have you been on? Or: how many good friends have you got in the world? Then we each take a piece of paper and a pencil and make a list. And whoever comes up with the most names is the winner. Three times my mother forgot a train from Prague to Budapest and a train from Lvov to Warsaw that we took with Manya. Then she forgot the bed in Bruges which was made of iron and had golden knobs, and where we had to lie so close that we didn't know any more which was me and which was my mother.

Beneath us there was a bar where people were dancing, and we thought our bed would start dancing too, or the floor would crack open, and all that laughing and shrieking would come into our room. For the people under us, our floor wasn't the floor, but the ceiling of the room they were in.

It was cold. My father sat on our little bed, sometimes on my leg, and spilled red wine over us. We were trying to go to Ostende then, but our travel money was only enough to get us to Bruges, and my father wanted to look at the churches there, and the dying quiet and the bewitched life.

The old liftboy says: 'We'll have to wire your father.' He lends me money for the telegram.

Now I'm going to the central post office; I know the way. There are crowds of people standing around everywhere, because the queen is riding by. I wouldn't mind seeing her myself, maybe she'll be wearing a big crown. But I don't have the time.

On the street there's a big German shepherd dog lying next to a beggar. The German shepherd has a picture of the queen strapped to its back, and on that she's certainly wearing a crown.

A man has painted his face all white. He crawls around on all fours, people sometimes give him money for that. I mustn't lose the money for the telegram. I wouldn't mind crawling around on all fours for a living.

Everywhere there are stalls with grapes, peaches, oranges and cake. I would so like to buy something. A lot of people are begging; probably they don't have any money either.

On the Damrak there's a little red box, with puppets jumping here and there and speaking – it's a play. In the distance there are people shouting and calling: 'Here comes the queen!' Little horses pull carriages with big

---

* Cf. Georges Rodenbach's novel *Bruges-la-Morte* (1892). (Trans.)

wardrobes made of gold and jewels. Music comes out of them. Music everywhere.

The nicest thing of all are the chestnut horses standing opposite the post office. They belong to the soldiers. I think I'm not allowed to feed the horses. One of them has a pink plaster on its leg. Maybe it got a little crazy and fell down; I should like to take a closer look. I've often fallen down myself, then my mother sticks plasters on me.

Opposite the post office is a sentrybox, which has a horse in front of it and a soldier mounted on it. The sentrybox is so big that the horse and man can walk in there.

I sent the telegram myself. I let the official help me. Now my father knows that without him we're sick and will surely die.

I think I've done something awful, but they were so sweet – the two guinea pigs. Maybe my mother will be pleased and recover her health.

I still had some money left over from the telegram. As I came out of the post office, I saw a very poor little boy, who had a white guinea pig, and then another one that was brown with black flecks. He showed them off to everyone, and sometimes got given some money. I terribly badly wanted to have the guinea pigs. I gave the boy all the money I had left. The boy even said they would have guinea pig babies. That way I'll have a hundred guinea pigs one day, and I can sell some. At last we're going to have money.

Now my mother's asleep. Her face is back to normal. Something awful happened. All at once my mother was not my mother any more. I thought she was the war and a bomb and about to blow up. I walked into the room, and she jumped out of bed, screamed and gave me a slap. She talked very fast and heatedly and wildly. I wasn't even able to tell her why I had been out for so long.

She thought my guinea pigs were rats, I wasn't able to explain anything to her. She flew to the telephone on the wall, she called all the people we know, and was furious with them; her eyes kept getting bigger and blacker. I didn't cry, I felt too scared.

She pushed all the bell-pushes in the room, yelled at the chambermaids and the room-service waiter. The waiter was to bring a shedload of food, and wine and cigarettes. She wanted to smoke – normally she never smokes.

She said she wanted to die, and then she picked up the telephone and called some more people and yelled at them. Her lips were trembling, her eyes kept getting more and more furious.

I sat huddled under the desk so she couldn't see me. One of my tortoises crawled past, my mother seized it. I wanted to scream – I thought she was going to hurl my tortoise out of the window or smack against the wall.

All at once my mother looked at the tortoise in her

raised hand, and her face went all small and tired-looking. She set the tortoise very gently on the ground, dropped on to her bed, and was asleep right away. Now I didn't feel afraid any more, I tucked my mother in so that her cold didn't get any worse.

My guinea pigs crawled off under the wardrobe. I wanted to play with them, but it was best not to bother them if they were going to have babies. That was something Herr Fiedler told me once, that you had to leave animals alone when they were going to have babies. I wonder why my tortoises don't get any babies, when I leave them alone so much of the time?

My mother is still asleep. I am very quiet. I'm playing with little silver balls on the carpet. You can't pick them up, they are like the most beautiful beetles in the world. Before, they used to be in the thermometer that was on the bedside table. Wherever you have a thermometer in my experience, you have sick people.

I wanted to break the thermometer, to see what was in it, and what makes it climb up that little tube, and then I broke it by accident – I cut myself a tiny bit. And suddenly the silver fever was running around the carpet in little balls.

Now my mother's going to get better, now I know what fever is. Now the carpet has fever, we're never going to have fever again, and I can play with the silver fever-beetles. Everything is lovely, and my father's coming back soon.

My mother's asleep, her hair is all golden, a pink-ish gold is shining into the room. Maybe I'm gold as well. Outside trams and motorcycles drive past. If I shut my eyes, it feels as if they're here in the room with me.

The table in our room has turned into a restaurant. The waiter came and spread a white tablecloth over it, and some glasses and wine and plates and so much food. My mother had ordered it, and now she hasn't drunk anything or eaten anything. She's asleep, she's changing back.

I don't like any of the food on the table. Maybe my guinea pigs would like it, though? I'm dying to look under the wardrobe, to see if they've had their babies yet. But I'd better not, otherwise the same thing will happen as happened with the fire-beans. Once I planted some fire-beans in a pot of earth so that they might make fire-flowers. Then I kept turning up the earth to see what was keeping the flowers. That way I disturbed the fire-beans so much that they never made any flowers.

My mother told me: 'You have to learn to wait and have patience. Things must be allowed to develop by themselves, everything must happen of its own volition.' Everything must happen of its own volition. I'm going to leave my guinea pigs in peace, and I'm not going to wake my mother.

There's a lovely coloured postcard under my mother's bed. It's from my father, and smells of my father. He writes: 'Kisses. Be patient. Courage.' And underneath that Manya wrote: 'Best wishes.'

When my mother woke up, she was better. Her eyes were mild and blue, her voice blew like a puff of soft wind across the room. She asked me: 'How many people did I call, how many people did I shout at? Oh dear, Kully, I must have been possessed!'

In not very many minutes, it's possible to offend an awful lot of people and make them angry with you. It takes much longer to talk them round afterwards. It's not even certain you'll succeed.

My mother's on the phone. She's not screaming any more, she's talking very softly, she wants everyone to forgive her. Well, she offended Herr Krabbe, and three poets who sometimes visited us. Also Frau Brühl, with whom we sometimes go and drink coffee. She was angry with me too, and gave me a slap, but I'm her daughter and I can't complain.

She's on the phone and curling her hair. She's on the phone and putting on the black silk dress with white lace trim. She's on the phone and powdering herself. She's shining and gleaming and smelling of violets. She kisses me very energetically and she's different again. 'I want to live, Kully, sweetheart, I love you – do you love me?' I always love my mother, only sometimes I worry about her.

She gets my guinea pigs out from under the wardrobe;

they haven't had any babies yet. There's a lot of food on the table, including lettuce. The guinea pigs are allowed to eat whatever they like.

My mother wants to feed the guinea pigs herself, but they are tired and would prefer to sleep and die. They lie down on our tablecloth all silky-soft. They aren't eating anything; maybe they're dead, or maybe they're having babies. You have to leave them in peace.

A black bird is flying in my mother's hair, which is her hat. She doesn't eat anything but drinks a glass of wine. The guinea pigs don't budge. I intended not to disturb them, but I carry them back under the wardrobe, and give them some lettuce leaves – maybe that'll bring them back to life.

My mother's going out, and says: 'Wait here for me.' She kisses me again. Her mouth is as soft and open as a bed with the corners turned back. But I'm not ready to go to sleep yet. My mother appears in the doorway. She's holding a piece of paper in her hand, a telegram form.

'I've already written a telegram, Mama,' I say. My mother stares at me, as if she hadn't understood what I was saying, then she hands me the telegram suddenly and says: 'No, I'm sending it; will you tear this up for me, Kully?' And she very quickly walks out. The telegram is addressed to Émile Jeannot, and it says: 'Yes, please come.'

On my mother's pillow are a letter and a picture of a man I don't know. He's like a real uncle, but not at all nice to look at. His eyes look sad, but maybe he was just tired. I always feel tired myself when I get my picture taken – it's too bad. The only people I know are the ones my parents see in the daytime. At night my parents meet many other people whom I never get to see, because I'm asleep.

I wonder whether I should rip up the letter and the picture. The man writes to my mother in French. Was she able to read it? Normally, I have to translate for her. What he writes is this:

Madame, I have never forgotten you. Do you remember how we were at the Viking in Paris a year ago, drinking champagne? You were beautiful and gay. Your husband had gone to Boulogne and left you in my care. I hope you weren't bored, Madame. A few days ago, I saw a mutual friend from Amsterdam. He has seen you. You are alone, he says, alone and unhappy. If you are in need of a friend, Madame, and a servant –

My mother comes back and takes the letter away from me. Her cheeks are flushed, and she has stuck some live carnations on her dress. She says Monsieur Jeannot is a friend of my father's too, and I ask her: 'Is he a writer as well?' My mother says yes, but he hardly ever writes novels, only poems. He is French, and he owns a French factory.

I like factories, with their purring machinery. It's too

bad that we know so few factory owners. And there are so many factories too. Once I saw a cigarette factory. Books are made in factories as well, but only after they've been written.

'What sort of factory does Monsieur Jeannot own, Mama?'

'Oh, don't ask so many questions, Kully,' says my mother. 'He has a coffin factory.'

If Monsieur Jeannot is a friend of my father's, perhaps he'll give us some coffins from his factory. Only what would we do with them? Perhaps when we're dead we can be buried in his coffins and not have to pay. What happens to all those dead people who don't have any money?

My mother said birds and other wild animals die too. What happens to all the dead birds? I remember a big forest where lots of birds were singing, but I didn't see a single dead bird lying around. Seagulls die too, and don't receive a burial. Where are all the dead seagulls and pigeons? Perhaps they fly up so high they never come down, and lie dead on the clouds. A lot of dead animals get eaten by people. At least those are accounted for.

A telegram arrives from my father. He is almost in Holland – he is in Belgium. The Dutch won't let him in, though, because he can't show them lots of money. They say they don't want to admit any more refugees. My mother and I can't stay here any longer either. But nor can we join my father in Belgium, because we don't have a Belgian visa.

My father brought a whole gaggle of people with him from Prague and Poland, where they were all living in fear. But we have just as much fear here. I wish my father was back. If he could travel as far as the Belgian border, and we travelled as far as the Dutch border, then we would at least be able to see each other, and wave. Herr Krabbe says if there's a war now, we'll all be locked up and shot.

A lot of people are coming towards us in the hotel lobby. We met them in Austria, in Prague, in Poland. Suddenly almost all of them are here in Amsterdam, and crying and saying: 'You're so lucky.' At that my mother starts crying too.

Outside the hotel is the big café, where people sit out in the open on wickerwork chairs and drink coffee. The lawn is a luminous green and everything looks shiny. The trams talk to the cars by shimmering and hooting and tinkling their bells. It's grown so warm, we don't need coats and rugs any more. If you give someone your hand, it's quite likely to stick to them. But soon it'll get colder again.

Sometimes my father rings from Brussels, and says: 'Be calm, children, be calm.' My father never cries.

It's warm and we're hungry. We can't leave, because we can't pay the hotel bill. We can't enter any other country, but we can't stay here either. Perhaps we'll be thrown into prison, and then we'll be fed.

Uncle Kranich is in prison too. We met Uncle Kranich in Vienna. Then he suddenly turned up here. He was old and fat, and wore a golden ring. My mother had a golden ring once, which we sold in Nice, because we were out of soap and toothbrushes. I don't really mind not having soap. But in big cities you get dirty very quickly, almost without doing anything.

Uncle Kranich would sit in our café with us in the sunshine, with a jaunty tie. He recited poems against the German regime, and so he was forced to leave Austria. Just like a Red Indian, he crawled across the border to Holland. Now he's being kept in prison. When he gets out, he won't be allowed to stay in Holland. He won't be allowed to enter another country either.

People tremble when they buy newspapers and magazines: what's going wrong with the world? I'd so much like to have another child to play with.

At night my mother holds me so tight it hurts me, and I can't sleep. So many cars are rushing past our window. 'Kully, I can't stand it any more,' my mother shouts, and she jumps out of bed, and orders a trunk call to Cologne. She wants to talk to my grandmother.

'Oh, Mama,' she cries, 'how are you? Everything is so awful!' I always thought of my grandmother as just my grandmother, but it seems she's also the mother of my mother.

My mother orders a huge breakfast up to our room; we eat till we're not hungry any more. Breakfast in Holland is enough for lunch and dinner. My mother says: it doesn't matter any more. She holds me tight, but in her mind she's somewhere else. She says words I don't understand and doesn't answer when I ask: 'Is it war?'

My mother doesn't even open the latest hotel bill. She's putting lovely curls in her hair. Sometimes she sits in the corner of the lobby, where there are glass tanks full of little fish that swim delicately and silently. Some of them look as though they have little lace trimmings as they stare at me out of their round eyes. Sometimes two fishes swim straight at each other, and kiss. That's the best.

There's a man with dark eyes who's often to be found at my mother's side. He holds her hand tight and kisses it. My mother's hand trembles slightly, like the fins of the littlest fish. Her eyes have become huge and blue.

She doesn't want to be alone ever. But my being with her isn't much help. Because I'm not able to talk about Mussolini and Hitler and Chamberlain, which are all names of various statesmen. That was all my mother was able to explain to me. But they're somehow all connected to the war. When I'm grown up, I'll be able to understand it. But what's the point of growing up, if it'll only make me sad? My mother said once that along with being grown up you become guilty; and there's nothing in the world as sad as being guilty.

I think what makes my mother saddest of all is not having my father with her. When my father's kissing her and stroking her hair with his hand, then she's always in a good mood. Sometimes now she wants to be lost to my father, and embark on a new life. Often she feels feverish and dead. Only my father's coming will make her live. It was never as bad as this.

Perhaps if war comes, we will never see my father again. That thought frightens my mother. She thinks he'll desert us and not love us any more. The café in front of the hotel already has soldiers in green uniform running around, but not with guns. Everyone thinks it will be war soon. They want to flee to America or Sweden, or they don't want anything at all, they just wait.

I'm not afraid, because I've got my mother with me. The waiter who brings us our breakfast in the morning has said he's not afraid either, and there isn't going to be any war. And if there is, and we are put in a camp, then he will continue to bring us our meals.

We know a Dutch family, because my mother used to go to the same boarding school as the Dutch woman, in Germany. They have two children. I don't get on with them at all, because they like screaming and hitting and pulling hair. I'd much rather play, myself.

Once I brought my doll's kitchen along to their house. My mother had given me an old blue silk blouse of hers, for us to make curtains and blankets out of. I also had some cigarette cartons to make furniture with, and silver paper to cut stars out of and lay on the blue carpet. That way we could have played heaven too.

But the children first laughed, then they screamed, and they jumped on my doll's kitchen and pulled my hair. I told them very calmly that if they did that again, I would have to take out my big pocket-knife and stab them.

And then the two of them went running to the grown-ups. The grown-ups weren't able to hear what they were saying, though, because they were listening to the wireless. There was a horrible yelling coming out of it that I really didn't like to hear. It was from Germany, and it was someone speaking about the war. The man who was speaking was Hitler. He wanted to have a new country, called Czechoslovakia.

When things got quieter, the Dutch woman wanted to go out and buy beans, lots and lots of beans, to eat with her children during the war. The children stopped pulling my hair, so I let them live. They were put to bed, and cried. Later, their father wanted to smack me, but I said he'd better not do that, otherwise I'd stab him as well.

Now I'm not allowed to consort with that Dutch family any more. My mother says she doesn't know what got into me. I don't think anything has got into me, myself, because I don't have a tummy ache. I won't stand having strange people and their children hitting and smacking me, when I'm a good girl and only try to play with them. My mother said once, you have to pay everyone back in the same coin, but you can't always do that. For instance, when the mosquitoes stung me in Italy, I couldn't sting them back. I could only squash them against the wall.

Didn't I say it, didn't I say it! My father's back.

My mother got up very early in the morning because of feeling so restless, and needing to see what was happening with the war. I huddled down in bed, where it was warm, rolled up like my guinea pigs (who really did have babies, but they were confiscated by the hotel management, the parents as well, and without me being paid a penny in compensation). I was thinking I might be able to make bookmarks out of cigarette packets and sell them on the street.

So there I was lying in bed, when the telephone rang. I didn't want to go, because this early in the morning it's usually Herr Tankaard. He wants to know whether my mother has got the cure for hair-loss yet, from Germany. Herr Tankaard writes poems but in Dutch, and he's always thinking about his hair because he hasn't got any. I would so like to sell him mine. But I think he wouldn't be able to transplant my hair. Anyway, he couldn't afford it.

When I picked up the phone, it was my father, speaking very fast. 'Not one word, Kully, you're not to tell anyone I'm here. Get in a taxi and go to the Pension Vandervelde.'

We had to go a very long way, past Vondelpark and

the Amstel. The streets got quieter, the houses smaller. When the taxi came to a stop, there was my father, pulling us out. 'Annie, call me Pierre; Kully, don't say Papa – best not to say anything at all till we're upstairs.'

He dragged us inside – the stairs were narrow, the passage was high and unlit, filled with a dreadfully fat woman in a yellow flowered dress. 'Can't have that,' said the woman, barring our way. Her stacked-up hair quivered on top of her head. 'No female company allowed in the bedrooms.'

'May I introduce Madame Vandervelde,' said Papa, 'a charming lady. But you would have even more charm and, dare I say it, sex appeal too, if you were to borrow some French savoir faire. If you should travel to France, Madame, then take my advice: if you want to appear honourable and trustworthy, then on no account stay in your hotel for longer than three days without receiving a young gentleman, or even an elderly gentleman, in your room. Even if it's just for the sake of appearances . . .'

My mother groans, the fat lady goes into a rage and yells: 'Don't forget you're in Holland now, and kindly follow Dutch customs.'

'But of course, Madame,' says my father, and all of a sudden he's terribly serious. 'Now don't force me to take extreme measures. Underneath my raincoat, I am completely naked. If you don't let us pass right away, I will be forced to take it off.'

My father drags my mother and me past the woman

and up the stairs. He unlocks the room, and says: 'Please see to it that we're not disturbed. Did I tell you, Madame, you remind me of Catherine the Great – you should have been a tsarina instead of marrying a building inspector. Stalin might have been your Potemkin, but you have expended your vast political energies on red velvet fittings. I know you're proud and good-hearted. And now you'll run out and fetch me a half-bottle of rum and something to eat, won't you, there's a dear. The little girl here is hungry, and I'm thirsty.'

'There,' says my father. He locks us into the room. 'Now either she'll bring masses of food, or else she'll be back with the police.'

Then we stand there in silence and look at each other. All of a sudden my father looks terribly pale and tired. He sits my mother down on the bed, and then he falls down. His head is on her knees. My mother lays both her hands on his hair.

There is silence. The room is small, cold, ugly, with no carpet. On the brown floor are some squeezed-out tubes of paint – blue, green, red. On a tiny wobbly table is a bunch of roses, and everything smells of dust and cellars. Under the roses there are seven little booklets. Hey, those are passports; we've got seven passports!

'Don't touch them, Kully,' calls my father. He's sitting on the bed next to my mother. He gives her a kiss and laughs. Then he gives me a kiss as well. He pulls on a shirt and a pair of trousers. He's laughing and talking.

There's a knock, and my father opens the door. Outside the door is a tray, which he picks up and brings inside. My father pours out a water glass full of rum for himself, while I start to eat. My father doesn't look quite so pale now, his hair doesn't look so sick and fibrous.

No one's to know that my father's here. He has an assumed name, and got into Holland on a Belgian passport. And he's not a writer any more either, he's a painter and interior decorator, but that's just pretend. He found some friends in Belgium who lent him their Belgian passports. Now he's loaning them on to some poor people who are not allowed to stay here any longer. With the Belgian passports they can get into France.

'Don't cry, Annie,' says my father. 'Everything'll be all right. I know, the times are worse than they've ever been. Really, I suppose I ought to murder you and Kully, and then kill myself – you're quite right. But you know I have absolutely no sense of responsibility. If there's war, then our prospects are zero, because the German publishers here won't print any more of our books. Don't even ask how I've been. And by the way, I don't think there will be war.'

My father no longer has a suitcase, but in a corner of the room is a big grey sack, from which he pulls sheets of paper covered in writing. Oh, I'm so relieved. At last we have the novel Herr Krabbe has been waiting for! My mother is twittering happily like a bird.

My father wants us to go straight back to the hotel.

My mother is to type everything up, then call Herr Krabbe, give it to him, and try all she can to get some more money out of him. My father doesn't have any money left, but he wants to try and borrow some from the fat woman.

'Stay in the hotel for the time being,' he says. 'Don't worry about a thing – I've thought ahead. Tomorrow morning I've asked a Dutch man to call you in Dutch and posing as an employee of the Amsterdam Bank. That will favourably impress the hotel, and soothe the nerves of the poor old management. You won't have to do anything, Annie, except stay on the phone and say "Yes" and "Thank you" at intervals, and at lunchtime ask the porter how long the Amsterdam Bank stays open. That will gain us time. Once the acute threat of war has abated, we'll have a better idea what to do.'

My mother is laughing, her eyes are big and blue. My father puts the seven passports away, because I'm not to play with them – not that I would have done. I am allowed to squeeze the tubes of paint out on the floor, though.

My father pulls coats out of the sack. 'Here's a sheepskin coat for you, Annie – I took it from Manya, who owns four furs. Manya is in Brussels too. Don't be jealous – she's there with Genek, they're back together. If you live with a volcano, be prepared for high temperatures. Indifference comes to a boil, and before long it's love once more.'

I get a coat too; it's from Madame Rostand, who crocheted it herself out of multi-coloured wool. It makes me look like a sofa cushion.

'Were you going to cheat on me, Annie?' asks my father. 'Did you allow that French coffin-maker to write you love letters? And squeeze hands with that young Dutch Romantic? I only wish you wouldn't be so abysmally stupid, Annie. You know you belong to me, and no one else. It's not in a man's interests to give a woman advice about love, but I'll make an exception for you: remember, Annie, that the only women who should take lovers are empresses or she-devils. Empresses, because they're in a position to have a bored or boring lover put to death; and she-devils, because they can induce a man to kill himself at the proper time.'

'But I haven't done anything,' says my mother, very *piano*, I think they call it. 'I love you, I was dreadfully lonely without you.'

'I know you haven't done anything, Annie, otherwise I would already have thrown you out of the window.' My father bangs his fist against the wall. I'm frightened and try to hide.

'My God, the child,' says my mother. 'Give some thought to the child and what she's going to make of all this.'

'Oh, Kully,' calls my father. He picks me up and throws me high in the air. 'Either the child will understand what I'm saying – in which case, it's not going to damage her.

Or she won't – and then at the very worst, it won't help her in later life.'

He plops me back down on the ground, and offers my mother some rum. She doesn't want any, so instead he makes her a ham sandwich. He tells her to take a bite of it, as if she were a little baby. Meanwhile, I am eating everything on the table in a completely grown-up and responsible manner.

My mother stands up. She wants to take me away and get to work on the manuscript. My father looks at my mother. 'Annie,' he says suddenly, 'is it true? I have the sense that I said goodbye to you a little too passionately in Brussels. Is it true, Annie?'

My mother says: 'Yes.'

My father pulls my mother down on the bed and sits next to her. Both are sitting perfectly still and astounded, like two plants under a shower of rain. What's going on now?

'We're going to have a baby, Kully,' says my father.

I don't know why we should have a baby now, all of a sudden, but my parents say there's nothing to be done about it. And it will cost money, money we don't have.

I am always afraid my parents might give me away one day. Frankly, I'd rather they gave away this new baby. I say: if push comes to shove, then they could just deposit it with Herr Krabbe at the publisher's.

'Not a bad idea,' says my father. 'The girl has some good ideas. A little nearer the time, Annie, you should go and see Krabbe; I know he's getting harder and flintier by the day – extraordinarily interesting, by the way, to observe the process of rapid petrifaction that so many people are going through nowadays – but I fancy he won't be equal to a woman in your condition. His other authors haven't put him to that particular test, so far as I know, so it'll be a new one on him. Don't worry yourself about it, Annie, everything will be taken care of, everything will be fine – I'll find a way. Even if they turn out to be Canadian quintupletsV – well, perhaps it's time to revive the idea of a trip to America.'

Everything's fine. My mother's laughing, my father's here. The promised baby is taking its time, and the war seems to be taking its time too. Perhaps it got lost somewhere on the way.

My mother doesn't toss and turn as much at night as she used to, and she doesn't scream in her sleep. There was one night before my father came to Amsterdam, when it was still Sunday on the street outside, cars were whizzing and people were singing, lights in the sky glittered into our room. I was lying in bed, but I wasn't sure if I was asleep or awake.

My mother sat bolt upright; I could only see her back, which was like a wall of pink silk. Sometimes a

---

* The Dionne quintuplets – all girls, born on 28 May 1934 – were the first known to survive beyond infancy. (Trans.)

little light flickered into our room, the telephone kept purring next door. Down on the street, a man was whistling a tune. My mother trembled: 'Did you hear that? Did you hear that whistling? That was the Horst Wessel Songo that someone was whistling in the street – here in Amsterdam.'

I don't know the song she means, but I wonder why it would make my mother so frightened and sad. I couldn't find her face any more, it was so far away. Then in my mind I changed my mother into a tree, because a tree is calm, a tree is unafraid. A tree doesn't get hungry, or cry. It doesn't laugh, and it doesn't talk. I turned her into a tree so that she would stop trembling. After that, I was able to sleep.

When I woke in the morning, I didn't wake her at first, but then I was scared she might be stuck as a tree. I combed her hair, pinched her big toe and changed her back into my mother.

We're going to go to Paris soon, and then we'll be somewhere else. And if we're somewhere else, we'll be one step further and happy. I always wake up long before my mother. I see the grey morning at the window. I raise my hand, waggle my fingers, and project shadows on the wall – hares and rabbits and giraffes.

Sometimes there's a bang on the street, but I can't tell if it was a gunshot or an exploding tyre, because I've

---

* Anthem of the Nazi party from 1930 to 1945. (Trans.)

never heard a gunshot. My father has a revolver he can shoot with. If we're ever really stuck, he'll shoot us with it. Then at least nothing more can happen to us. Probably you smell bad when you're dead, just like my dead sea creatures did, but that doesn't matter because we won't be able to smell ourselves.

Grown-ups were trying to tell me how it's possible to go to heaven. I hate it when people have such a low opinion of children that they think they'll believe anything they're told. What person in their right mind would stay in the world with worries and strife if he could be in heaven instead, and it not even cost any money?

Nor do I believe that bad people go to hell. Bad people are much too canny to do bad things if they knew they would go to hell as a result. My father was talking to some Dutch people once, and he said: 'It might be nice for a change if they started preaching that all the good people will go to hell, and all the evil people will go to heaven. Then the good people would go bad, and the bad people wouldn't have any victims any more. Perhaps the world would be a more peaceful place as a result.'

That made the Dutch people angry, and they said they were implacable men of faith, and they called my father a heretic with no fear of God, and who would end up contaminating my soul too. My father said it was all right to be implacable or to have faith – but a combination of the two was as disgusting as anything he could think of.

'As for fear of God? Why? Why not trust in God? I'd

rather my little girl worshipped matchboxes or liqueur glasses than that she be afraid of God. Everything that's wrong with the world begins with fear. I don't see why people have to think of God as a modern dictator, who makes people run around in circles in muzzles and handcuffs. All that mess in Germany could only result because the people there have lived in fear for ever. No sooner is a child born than fear of its mother and father is instilled in it. And then it has to honour its father and mother as well. Why? Either you love your parents, in which case you honour them as a matter of course, or you don't love them, in which case your honouring them isn't going to do them a blind bit of good. First a father demands that his child be afraid of him. Then there's school and fear of the teacher, fear of God at church, fear of military or other superiors, fear of the police, fear of life, fear of death. Finally, the people are so crippled and warped by fear that they elect a government that they can serve in fear. Not content with that, when they see other people who are not set on living in fear, they get angry, and try in their turn to make them afraid. First of all they made God into a kind of dictator, and now they don't need Him any more, because they've come up with a better dictator themselves.'

I'm not afraid of God. And I'm not afraid of my father either, even though he has a bad temper sometimes. I know he'll always be good again.

*

I am glad I don't have to go to school any more. You really don't learn anything at school, I find. The Dutch children I know are much bigger than I am. But I can speak much better English, Polish, French and German than they can. Only their Dutch is a bit better than mine.

I can also follow the exchange rates in the newspaper, and convert guilders into zlotys, and zlotys into Belgian francs. That's the most important aspect of mathematics. You must know that having ten dollars is a thousand times better than having one mark. The children here are really dim, not to know that.

The other day they had an atlas which was full of pictures, not real pictures but drawings of various blobby shapes in blue and green and pink. Those were meant to be countries, and the children were supposed to study them for school. In reality, all those countries look nothing like that, and most of them I've seen for myself, so I know. And I expect we'll get to see the remaining ones in time too.

The children don't believe me when I say I've been on a sleigh in the Carpathians with my father and a Polish hunter, and have lain on a fur in a hut and eaten bear steaks. Nor do they believe what my English friend writes from London, which is that the fog has grown so thick and black that he could break off a piece of it and pack it in a parcel to send me.

I can read very loud now, because I'm always reading from the newspaper to my mother as she gets dressed.

I don't like newspapers, because they are usually full of nasty things: about unattended children falling into boiling water, or seventy-year-old men who are crushed by lorries, or women who are driven demented and chop up their families with an axe.

My father says the extermination of one's family is a silly modern fad, like painting your fingernails scarlet. He doesn't like bright red lacquered nails on women, because they look like bleeding chunks of meat and put him off his food and drink. He once told a lady the only way he could stand her red fingernails was if she set them off with a ruby in her belly button, which the lady refused to do. Mind you, I don't see how you can fix a ruby in your belly button anyway.

It's almost Christmas again. Here in Holland Christmas isn't such a big deal, because they have something called Sinter Klaas beforehand, where children get given presents and walk around with lanterns in a procession and sing. If we're still here at Sinter Klaas, I might join the procession this year. I could buy myself a lantern and all. Now that my father's here again, I can always find money under his bed. There is Dutch money which is so small you almost can't see it. But it's pretty valuable, you get quite a lot for it.

My father is still staying at that dangerous fat woman's house. She now has those red-lacquered fingernails because my father kisses her hand. He doesn't say anything about her nails, because she always buys him rum and lets my mother stay with him sometimes, and a woman like that is able to take some liberties. My father always kisses women on the hand. My mother used to object to it, until my father said: 'A man who doesn't kiss other women's hands won't kiss his own wife's feet.'

In Germany we always spent Christmas at my grandmother's, which was lovely. There was a Christmas tree set up in the dining room with lights and gleaming balls, and a white star on its very tip. We sang a song together, and everyone thanked everyone else for their presents.

Then I was allowed to eat as much cake and marzipan as I wanted. My father got restless, and wanted to go to a pub and drink a glass of beer, because he doesn't like being shut up inside people's flats. But all the pubs were shut. Also, the trams weren't running. I suppose my father didn't really like Christmas that much. He doesn't care for singing.

The lady with the bird's nest once expressed surprise at that, and said: 'Where there's singing, join the throng – only bad people have no songs.'

Then my father said that was exactly the throng you shouldn't join, because where there was singing there was the greatest danger. People singing together was halfway to murder; there wasn't a war that didn't start with singing.

When it was Christmas last year, we took the Pullman train from Amsterdam to Paris. I'm not so keen on

Pullman trains; they're so expensive, we don't really know how we came to be on one. Nor can you run around in them, because they really just consist of a restaurant. They don't have any compartments or corridors.

But it's true that customs inspectors are more considerate with the luggage on Pullman trains than on normal trains. It's also easier to get a Belgian transit visa on them. Also, all the railway employees know us. My father has some great friends among them. They come running up to his table, and bring him something called Marc de Bourgogne, which is a kind of cognac that is supposed to give him a foretaste of Paris.

Even on ordinary trains, my father likes to sit in the dining car, but it's not so easy there. Especially on French trains, they want people to eat up and clear off. They don't like you to sit for hours over your food. It makes my father mad when people start sweeping up around him, and I can understand his irritation, because it makes everything dirty.

My father is an especially good friend of one of the Pullman waiters, because they were together once when some famous politician from Catalonia or Pentagonia was travelling on the train as well. All at once there was a huge bang. Everyone thought a bomb must have fallen on the politician. He probably thought so himself, because they have a lot of that sort of thing wherever it is he comes from.

But then the *chef de train* had to apologize profusely, because it was only a heating pipe that had blown up. My father loves it when things like that happen. The waiter was very amused as well.

For Christmas the waiter gave my father a big wooden Christmas tree he carved himself. It wouldn't fit in any of our suitcases, and so my father had to carry it under his arm. There was no question of giving it to anyone or leaving it somewhere. Of course the waiter knew perfectly well that the tree wouldn't fit into any of our suitcases. If he didn't see it, he would know right away that we didn't have it any more.

Sometimes my father hates the tree and says how the best friendships can be ruined by presents: it was best if I never gave any presents to anyone, ever. It's difficult getting rid of stuff anyway; that's why we have so much luggage.

Old shoes are the most trouble. You can't wear them any more, because they're already too broken, and you can't give them to anyone either. On two occasions, we just left them behind in the hotel room. That was really very stupid of us. Both times, a boy came running up to the train with the shoes, and we had to give him a tip, with money that we didn't really have to give.

What's best with things like that is to wedge them under the hotel mattress, when usually they'll only be discovered when the train has gone. But you can only do that if you haven't left a forwarding address at the hotel, because otherwise they might put them in a parcel, and you might even end up having to pay duty on them.

That happened to us once in Italy, with a pile of completely filthy and torn shirts. Of late, I've taken to secretly dropping things like that in some corridor somewhere. It makes me feel as nervous as if I was stealing. Even when what I'm doing is actually the opposite.

When we arrive in Paris, my father is always so happy that he starts dancing at the Gare du Nord. Paris is his favourite city in the whole world. Other places my father can stand for four weeks at the most, yet he can be in Paris for three months, but then that's it.

Really the only time we're happy is when we're on a train. No sooner have we arrived in a city than we feel this terrible panic we may never be able to leave. Because we never have any money, we feel imprisoned by any hotel in any city, and from the very first day we think of our liberation.

The last time we arrived in Paris, it was snowing silently and softly. We took a taxi to our hotel on the Boulevard Saint Germain. The Place de la Concorde gleamed with silvery light. Outside the cafés stood little iron stoves; people sat on light wickerwork seats round them and drank red, green, blue or brown drinks. My father wanted to go out immediately.

In the hotel my father threw his arms around the

concierge, whose name is Anatole and who has a horrible squint and knows lots of things, in particular about the deals that my father makes with Herr Krabbe. Before he sets his name to them, my father likes to discuss them with Anatole.

Whenever we go anywhere, my mother looks out of the windows at the station as the trolleys full of books are pushed past. She wants to see whether any of my father's are among them. My father isn't so interested in whether his books are finding buyers. What's more important to him is Anatole saying he can't make head or tail of Herr Krabbe's royalty statements.

Herr Fiedler and his wife were standing in the hotel lobby when we arrived. They had thought we might be there. They were just trying to pay us a visit.

'Don't be alarmed,' said Frau Fiedler. 'Jeanne Moth is here.'

'Oh, my God,' said my mother.

'Oh, how wonderful,' said my father.

Anatole brought some Calvados for all the grown-ups to drink. I got a squishy banana. The valet took the luggage up in a lift with the taxi driver. Anatole paid the driver, sat down with us and had a tiny bit to drink. Herr Fiedler drank nothing at all, and my father drank an awful lot.

Then they talked endlessly about Jeanne Moth. Jeanne Moth is a woman from Germany, who's not going back there either. She paints and takes pictures, and also she's been to America. I saw her in Ostende one time. She has terribly wild dark-red hair and a big red mouth. She is restless, runs back and forth the whole time, and laughs and cries and talks. But once I saw her sitting on the beach, all mute and silent.

'She can be quite charming, but mostly she's enervating,' says Herr Fiedler.

'That depends on your nerves,' said my father. 'I like her myself.'

'Yes, because she stays up all night drinking with you,' said my mother.

'She can't leave any man in peace,' exclaimed Frau Fiedler.

'Oh the contrary,' said my father. 'Her instincts are so finely honed, she flirts exclusively with those men with whom she senses she has a chance.'

Frau Fiedler flushed and got angry: 'Ach, as if that was so hard, turning some man's head, if what you are is shameless. A fool will always be found if there's a willing seductress. Every man is vain enough to fall for that.'

'She does not need to have recourse to crudity to make herself unpopular,' said my father.

My mother gets angry too: 'If you ask me, I think she's cold and calculating.'

'Nonsense,' said my father. 'She's capable of the blindest teenage crushes on the least appropriate subject or object, and of giving up more than she can possibly afford.'

'She rang my husband three times yesterday,' called Frau Fiedler, 'and showered him with praise for his latest book. There's not a writer in the world who's capable of withstanding that.'

'More importantly, no writer's wife should be capable of withstanding it,' said my father.

But Frau Fiedler was getting more and more excited: 'She has a bad character.'

Then all at once Jeanne Moth is standing by the table; her hair is redder than ever. She laughs with pleasure and gives me a kiss, and to Frau Fiedler she says: 'Oh, my dear, I'm so happy to hear you say that. There's nothing worse for a woman than to have her good character praised by other women. This morning I thought I was looking so old and ugly, I had dreadful feelings of inferiority, but now –'

She kisses my father: 'Peter, my angel, how long is it since we last saw each other? I don't recall having seen that tie. How's your work? And when are we going to go for a walk? I have so many things to tell you about, I need your advice . . . Have I changed very much?'

She kisses my mother: 'Lord, am I happy to see you! You look lovely, Annie. You're as slim as a little girl now. See what disgusting creases I've got on my brow. And I've got a hole in my stockings as well – I haven't been able to buy a new pair for days. Were you having a go at me as well? I do wish you wouldn't. I think your husband is delightful. But he doesn't care for me.'

She waves her big grey hat this way and that. I get excited and feel tired. Suddenly it's as if there were a thousand people in the lobby. She drops into a dark green velvet armchair, which my father has pulled up for her. 'Just for a moment. I must go. Anatole, aren't you going to give me a drink? Were you attacking me as well?'

'I don't hate anyone, and I don't attack anyone,' said Anatole, pouring. 'A little one or a big one?'

'Big one.' She knocks it back in one gulp: '*A votre santé*!' Her hand is very white. She has a black ink stain on the thumb.

'God, I'm so glad you've come, Peter. Hey, he's a Norwegian, about fifty, grey hair and sweet blue eyes like a sleepy baby, and he never goes anywhere without his umbrella. What do you think? His wife is terribly nice, a pink ball of suet. I hope she won't be jealous. But they've been married for fifteen years, I just met them in Oslo. Now they're over in Paris for the very first time, so touchingly innocent. A week ago, I had to have a molar extracted. Does it notice when I laugh? I mean, does it bother a man very much if a woman is missing a tooth, or could you love her anyway – Fiedler? Your new book is magnificent. If you come to the Deux Magots tomorrow afternoon for an aperitif with me, I'll tell you some wonderful things, and take your picture for a New York magazine. Goodbye, darlings. Gotta dash, mustn't keep my Norwegians waiting.'

And suddenly she's gone, so quickly you're not quite sure if she was there at all.

No one speaks. Then Frau Fiedler says: 'And now she's making that poor Norwegian woman unhappy. One should really see to it that she leaves France; something should be done about her. She's a German émigrée, and she has no *carte d'identité*. Her French visa ran out a week ago, she told me so herself.'

'That's enough!' yells Herr Fiedler. His eyes are flashing with anger.

'Ah,' says my father, 'I do miss the good old days when nice middle-class women would hit each other over the head with umbrellas when they were jealous of each other – and where less pleasant women would write nice anonymous letters! Nowadays even the nice ones resort to political backstabbing. Politics really seems to have poisoned all manner of people and all manner of personal relations. Jeanne is such a nice girl, sometimes a little over-fond, a little confused and a little prodigal with herself and her emotions. She's sensible all right, but give her a chance to do something silly, and you can bet she will. But there's not a mean bone in her body.'

My father gets up, puts his hat on, offers no one his hand, and goes off. Herr Fiedler picks up his hat and runs off after him.

My mother is crying. Frau Fiedler shakes her head and says: 'Well, do you understand what just happened there?'

Anatole says: '*Mais oui, madame.*' And then he disappears behind his porter's desk, and unhooks our key from a blackboard and says: *'Elle est fatiguée, la petite.'*

I would so like to run behind the porter's desk, and see all the things that are kept there, but my mother's crying and I'm tired. I fall asleep in the lift.

When I woke up, I was lying with my mother in an especially big bed. She was still crying, the chambermaid brought in a big bowl of milky coffee and some croissants, and my father wasn't back yet. Then my mother telephoned my grandmother, because it was Christmas, and because my father was away.

At lunchtime Jeanne Moth came running into our room in leaf-green pyjamas and no slippers, and undressed right away and sat in the bath and comforted my mother from there. Later we all got dressed very quickly and went out together with the Norwegian couple to look for my father.

We found him in the Coupole, even though that's such a huge café it's impossible to find anyone there. Everything is muddled together, there are unbelievable numbers of people, and in some cases you can't even tell if someone is a man or a woman. Everyone laughed, and it was all fine.

My mother had to eat practically a whole turkey, and my father wanted to eat oysters and snails at the same time, and the Norwegians wanted some *choucroute garnie*, because nowhere has such good sauerkraut as France. And my grandmother always thought of sauerkraut as something German. I had to eat rice and an awful lot of cake. It was Christmas.

Outside, the clouds turned into pink gold, and sunshine dropped from them on to the hard cold paving stones. Pink and blue lights swam up from the cafés and cinemas and houses opposite, and it got to be a very light evening in quite a hurry, because really it was still afternoon.

The Norwegian man kept gazing at Jeanne Moth, and she fluttered her eyelashes at him, and gazed back, and didn't speak.

'I'm just glad,' said the round Norwegian woman, and caressed my mother's face with her hand, which was like a pudgy pink cushion. 'If you come to Paris for the very first time, you're under its spell and you fall in love. I'm just pleased for my old man that he's still capable of something like that. And I'm pleased to have a husband who's attractive to a nice pretty woman like Jeanne. I'm afraid I can no longer manage to seduce one of the thousand faithful husbands who are waiting to be seduced.'

'Well, you have seduced me, Madame,' said my father and he bought some red roses from a pale woman, and a rattling wooden snake from a short, funny-looking man. He gives the snake to my mother, and I take it away from her immediately, because I'm the one who needs toys like that, so I can play fakir or snake-charmer and circus with it.

Jeanne Moth wants to leave; she has a big suitcase that

she took with her from the hotel, and she hasn't said why. The Norwegian man picks up his umbrella in one hand and Jeanne Moth's suitcase in the other. We walk through Montparnasse, which in our language means something a bit like heaven.

Just in the place where there are most lights shining on the street and the people, Jeanne clicks the lock of her suitcase while the Norwegian man is carrying it. The suitcase falls open, and clothes and scarves and necklaces tumble out. People stop and laugh, and Jeanne laughs as well. Her hair goes wild again, and a moment ago it was really quite tame. And she picks up the things off the ground to give them to the people who are standing around us. The people look surprised and deadly serious, and don't want to accept anything.

'Never mind,' says Jeanne, and she throws everything in a heap, and tramples on it, and says 'Forget it' to my father when he tries to pack it all up again, and pulls him violently away, and flings the empty suitcase against the wall of a house.

'Jeanne,' says my father, 'Jeanne, you're drunk – be sensible.'

'No,' she says, 'I'm not drunk, or if I am, then I'm drunk out of sheer sobriety – or the only time I'm sober is when I'm drunk. Leave me be, Peter. I always want to do something good, but I have no patience, and if you want to do something good without patience it turns out bad, and I'm impatient in love and impatient in hate, and

I have no patience with life and no patience with myself.'

After that she doesn't say anything, none of us says anything, and we head back to the hotel. Once she reaches for my hand, but I'm scared. Far away, where she left her suitcase and her belongings lying, there are now a lot of people shouting, and a policeman stalks into their midst. I can see him, and I want to run back and see what happens next, but my mother holds my hand tight and pulls me along.

That evening in the hotel Jeanne is suddenly dead, because she wanted to be dead. I don't know how she did it. I don't think it's at all a terrible thing, because what's the point of living if you could just as well be dead? But the grown-ups thought it was awful, and no one took any interest in me any more. I played with my wooden snake.

The Norwegian couple left, saying they didn't like Paris and they didn't like Christmas either. My father wrote Jeanne's mother a letter with a shaking hand and a clear brow, and my mother sealed the envelope and stuck a stamp on it, and took it to the post office. And Anatole went and got a doctor and then a whole lot of policemen. Later on, the Fiedlers turned up, and Herr Fiedler said: 'What a terrible thing, what possessed her to do it? She had so much talent.' And Frau Fiedler said: 'Perhaps it's for the best.'

Then all at once Jeanne Moth was alive again. The doctor came out of her room and told everyone about it. Pretty soon, she was running around again, and the grown-ups all got excited, but my mother and I were distracted, because just then my grandmother arrived in Paris.

My grandmother was allowed to take out money from Germany to go to Italy with, and she wanted to take my mother and me to Italy with the money, so that we could be together, and live for three weeks on no money. My grandmother is big and round, with hair like a fat white bonnet. She needs to be kept away from my father, because otherwise she will attack him. She is the only woman in the world who doesn't get on with my father, and my father is afraid of her too.

At first, my father didn't want us to go to Italy, because Italy is friends with Germany, which makes it a dangerous place to visit. But we are émigrés, and for émigrés all countries are dangerous. Lots of ministers make speeches against us and no one wants to have us in their country, even though we're not at all harmful and in fact just like other people.

There are also some émigrés who are not writers. Émigrés form clubs or associations where they can squabble in peace. A lot of émigrés want to die, and my father often says that's the best and only way out, but they are all a bit indecisive and aren't sure how to go about it, because it's not enough to just pray: dear Almighty God, please can I be dead tomorrow.

I mean, Jeanne Moth wanted to be dead, and it didn't

work out in her case either, which shows that it can't be that simple. In the end, all she came away with were a lot of expenses that she couldn't afford. Then she carried on living illegally, without a visa in Paris, but even if someone had denounced her and the police had come for her, even then she wouldn't have been certain that they would have taken out their pistols and shot her dead.

Most people have to do their dying without help all by themselves, and there's always the danger that someone might save them. When I'm grown up, I want to be dead too, but there's a lot of time till then.

My father said he was killing himself gradually and was doing all sorts of things to shorten his life, including smoking an awful lot of cigarettes with black tobacco in them, and drinking thousands of drinks in all the colours of the rainbow. It doesn't seem to kill him, but it does sometimes make him laugh.

Coming from Germany, my grandmother talked about Germany, which makes my father unhappy. My grandmother is well meaning, and always brings presents, but she doesn't understand about things. I don't understand about them either, so I'm careful not to talk to her, in case she turns out to be an enemy and denounces us. It seems well-meaning people bringing presents can sometimes be enemies, especially if they live in Germany. My father's forever saying we mustn't trust anyone.

*

One time in Paris I went in the afternoon with my father to Charlie's, which is a bar. Charlie is the barman, and a friend of my father's. There weren't any other customers; I was sat in a corner, and Charlie was in a hurry to finish a bottle of cognac with my father, because it was too good for ordinary customers, so he was going to fill the bottle with inferior cognac once it was empty.

My father understood that right away, and I had to keep terribly quiet and not disturb them. Afterwards Charlie was going to take a Pyramidon tablet, but ended up swallowing a fifty-centime piece by accident instead. After that he was crying about how wicked people were, and my father was crying too. They were both inconsolable.

Then my mother and my grandmother came along. My grandmother wasn't crying; instead she was giving little coughs of disgust, and wanting to leave on the night train to Italy immediately. And that's what she did too. My mother and I were supposed to go with her, but we ended up missing the train because of me.

I went for a little walk around Paris, and first looked at the thousand bird cages on the Seine, and then outside a bistro I saw a man making huge towers and trees out of one single newspaper. I followed the man until I didn't know where I was. On the way I got some visiting cards printed for my mother on the street, because I was so curious to see it done, but then I didn't have any money to pay for them, and I promised to come back later.

Because of that I couldn't have taken the night train anyway.

In the evening my father was in a state of great excitement, because a friend of his had taken his life. He wasn't even an émigré but a French cobbler, and he was a big fat jolly man, but he couldn't stand his wife and daughters because they kept scolding him and laughing at him, and wanting money from him all the time, and telling him he couldn't drink Pernod. It looks like green milk, and tastes like liquid aniseed cookies, if you can imagine that, but it still isn't a suitable drink for children.

First the cobbler was drinking Pernod with my father, and then he had strife with his family, and to annoy them he quickly cut up his hands, and his wife was furious because he'd sat on their best sofa, and got his blood all over it, and ruined it. My father was very upset. I think it would be best if people couldn't be born any more.

The following evening my mother and I left the Gare de Lyon on a beautiful train to join my grandmother in Italy. My father gave the conductor some money to treat us well, and there were some very serious agreements entered into. We were to write from Italy every day, and at the end of fourteen days we were to go to Nice and wait for my father there.

Wagons-lits are the best things in the world, and I prefer the top bunk. My mother was very excited and kept saying, 'We're going South.' I suppose that means she's never been there.

In the morning when we woke up, the whole world was different. The sky was three times as big and three times as high as anywhere else, and it was such a brilliant blue that it hurt your eyes. We passed bare-looking mountains with strange black and silver trees growing on them.

My mother was so excited she couldn't eat any breakfast in the dining car. I was terribly hungry. All the time my mother was pointing out things to me that I could see perfectly well for myself. Spring flowers were blooming in little gardens, and the sun was almost white.

We got off the train at Marseilles to go to a hotel near the port to meet a Swiss friend of my father's, who is very rich because, rather than write books, he sells watches. My mother was to persuade him to start a literary magazine with my father as editor, and give him the money for it. But in our experience rich people have always turned out to be really tight-fisted and mean, and never hand over their money, which I suppose is how they got to be rich in the first place.

We climbed down white terraces to Cannebière, and walked in silence. The world was new, people here lived faster and brighter lives. In the harbour, the sea glittered like blue ice; our hearts thumped, we felt so happy it scared us, and the air had the wild and damp smell of the bottom of the sea.

Behind frail crooked houses blew scraps of brightly

coloured laundry, Negro soldiers passed us in red caps, a small grey donkey pulled a big cart, dirty children played and leaped like rubber balls, and when a ship hooted in the harbour, I thought it was laughing. My mother said: 'I feel happy.' She looked so tiny under that gigantic big brilliant sky.

In Paris, the sky was sometimes like a blanket, and when I looked at a cloud, I could pull it down to me in my imagination, and let it warm me, but here there were no clouds, and you could never reach the brilliant blue sky with the white sun, so I shivered. I don't think I felt this cold even in Poland.

Outside the restaurants there were baskets piled high with oysters and strange sea creatures I didn't know. Some of them were maybe plants, but as with everything like that, I expect it looks nicer than it tastes. I saw a lot of damp little hedgehog-like things in the baskets; some of them had been cut open, and their insides were all red. I asked my mother to taste some of them for me, but she wouldn't, she didn't know how.

We sat in the hotel restaurant, which consisted only of bare glass walls, like an aquarium, so we could see the harbour and the ships. Waiters carried big glistening fish this way and that, and a little wizened brown man from the hotel management gave my mother and me sticky sweets because he knew my father.

My father's Swiss friend was there as well. He was thin and dried out and had a small brown leather purse with a zip. My father would have known right away that a man like that wouldn't give money, not to start a literary magazine, and not for anything else either.

I kicked my mother under the table a bit, but she didn't understand, and wasted a lot of time quite needlessly on that silly man. She ordered bouillabaisse, which is a kind of soup that's made out of the Mediterranean; all the creatures in the Mediterranean float around it in a hard-to-identify way, and some of them of course are poison-ous. When people have had enough of life, they can choose to die either by mushrooms or bouillabaisse, but in either case I think they have to order it specially from the hotel kitchen.

Some young Americans were sitting at the next table, drinking champagne, and waving their hands and talking loudly all at once. The Swiss man kept looking at my mother with his ill-looking green eyes. He wanted to be nice to her and treated her to a bottle of Vichy water, and said: 'You must have been very beautiful when you were younger.'

All at once my mother became silent and annoyed. I couldn't understand why, and nor could the Swiss man either. The white sun was suddenly burning red. It dropped into the sea, which caught fire and burned with wild flames.

The Swiss man was reflecting sadly. He was sad about all the money that a literary magazine would cost, and that he had no intention of parting with so much. He wanted to treat my mother to a second bottle of Vichy water and press her hand consolingly, but my mother didn't feel in the mood for that. The flames in the sea turned golden red. Her hair gleamed like the song sung by a man on the street. The singing beat against the high windows, and asked to be admitted.

The sea extinguished the sun, and turned shiny and black. The little tan hotel manager brought my mother a large bouquet of yellow mimosas. Their soft scent wafted across the table, my mother was happy again. That night, when my father telephoned from Paris, she stroked the earpiece.

The following evening, we left for Italy and my grandmother. 'Do you know the land where the lemon trees bloom?' asked my mother. 'That's where we're going now.' And we did go there, but I didn't see any blooming lemon trees.

Ventimiglia is the Italian border, and I straight away lost my temper with the Italians. What they like to do is take travellers' passports and disappear off with them into a gloomy station hall. What for? At first I thought they wanted to steal our passports. My mother was so worried, her hands were cold and slippery.

We wanted to go straight on to my grandmother, in Bordighera, but those Italians made us miss our train. They gave us back our passports, but you just knew they would have liked to keep everyone's passports. I wanted to scream and stamp my feet, but my mother told me I mustn't do that on any account.

Then it got wonderful like in a fairytale book. We drove to Bordighera in a horse-drawn carriage. It was cold and dark, and our coachman gave us blankets to cover ourselves with. The horse was brown and tired, and kept stopping. And when it did trot along, the carriage didn't want to go, and kept lurching and almost falling over. My mother wanted to protect me by keeping firm hold of me. We couldn't yet speak any Italian, but my mother was happy that the coachman addressed her as 'Signora'.

We drove past more bare-looking mountains. When I saw a dark green tree with live oranges hanging from it, I fell right out of the carriage, but I didn't hurt myself. I ran over to the tree and touched the oranges and still couldn't believe it. Otherwise I would have picked some. The coachman had let the horse run on, and my mother had to shout for a long time before he made it stop. I ran after the carriage, and by the time I was sitting in it again, the horse was being bolshy again.

In Bordighera we went first to the station, but my grandmother wasn't there. We needed to find her, because we didn't have any money except for the Bottom Dollar. The Bottom Dollar was a ten-dollar note, which my mother kept in her knickers for emergencies, and must never be spent.

Then we had to look for my grandmother in the hotel.

The horse disliked street corners, and didn't want to turn left or right, but only go in a straight line. That meant driving past sea cliffs, almost as far as Ospedaletti, whose lights we saw glittering in the distance. And a little way above it was a glimmering garden of stars and light. That was San Remo, the coachman shouted out over his shoulder.

After a long time and a difficult search, we found my grandmother in a hotel my father would never have set foot in, because it was a family-run pension where they rang bells when it was mealtime.

It wasn't easy for me to pick up Italian in Bordighera, because to begin with I encountered almost no Italians. Almost all the people there were German, and they spoke German too. The nearest most of the Germans got to speaking foreign was that they said German words with a French or Italian accent.

I paid very close attention, but what I learned first in Bordighera was not Italian but Berlinian. That only came to light later, and I really wasn't to know, because Berlinian was completely foreign to me; it's quite a different type of German from Kölsch. In Poland I once had the experience of speaking very good Polish, only to learn that it wasn't Polish at all, but Yiddish. It's not hard to speak a foreign language; what's harder is identifying which one it is. To this day, I have the hardest time keeping my Chinese from my Japanese.

Those people in Bordighera who weren't German were ancient Englishwomen, who always wanted to grab me when I was on my way to play, and ask me about Hitler. I don't know the man, but my father doesn't like him. When I'm grown up, I expect I'll find out what's wrong with him.

What I do know is that Hitler belongs to the Germans, but the Italians have one of their own, called Mussolini. The Germans in our Italian pension were forever praising and admiring Mussolini. In return, the Italians praised and admired Hitler. My mother sometimes praises the children of other mothers, and in return the other mothers have to praise me. They usually manage, but I know they often don't like me much.

My grandmother doesn't like Hitler much either, but she's afraid of him. She always has to go home to Germany, and then she might be locked up, for having been with us. She's never able to speak out. Germans are not supposed to speak out; they're supposed to listen to the radio instead.

My grandmother was always speaking to my mother in whispers. At first I really thought they were secrets, and I wanted to hear them. Yet they weren't secrets at all, but stuff like butter being very hard to get hold of in Germany. And before that, my grandmother would say things like: 'Oh, Annie, it is really high time we had a frank exchange.'

And then they talked about butter for Lord's sake, and

just for that we had to travel so far and meet in Italy. Sometimes I'm not sure whether I don't understand grown-ups, or if they're just too stupid for words.

My mother saw silk nighties in Bordighera and dreamed about them because they were so lovely and such good value. She loves my father, she loves my grandmother, and she loves me. But right after me she loves silk. And sometimes she loves silk more than she loves us people.

My grandmother needed all her money to get us through the days, and she didn't want to buy any silk nighties. My mother wanted to change the Bottom Dollar, because you could get so many lire for it. And she wanted to do it secretly.

She gave it to a German man who was our neighbour at table, and had a friendly face with surprised eyes like blue marbles. He drank Chianti, the Italian wine, out of straw bottles, and it made him ill so that he had to drink Fernet Branca afterwards, which is an Italian digestif. He was always smiling a gentle bold smile, and spoke very little and rather unclearly.

My grandmother had got into conversation with him, because he was from Cologne as well: a dentist, who wanted to enjoy a peaceful holiday, and who liked complaining with my mother about the bad meals at our pension.

Because he spoke favourably about Hitler, my mother at first didn't want to get into conversation with him, but because of my grandmother she couldn't criticize Hitler either, and also because Italy is potentially dangerous. And my grandmother found him so innocent and touching and confidence-inspiring. She wished my mother could have found a husband like that, especially once he suddenly stopped drinking Chianti.

In the evening, my mother gave the touching gentleman her ten-dollar bill, because he asked to have it so that he could go and change it for her in the morning. He kept looking at my mother with trembly eyes. My grandmother was pleased because he obviously found my mother so beautiful and attractive. I didn't like him myself, because he was as shaky as an old fruit-machine. Even when he was sitting perfectly still, he was doddering away to himself. If it wasn't his head that was doddering, it was his eyes. He was an ugly doll, a stupid fruit-machine.

When we returned to the pension at lunchtime after a morning by the sea in the hot sun, the blue-eyed man had skedaddled to France – with our ten-dollar bill. To begin with, my mother didn't want to tell my grandmother anything, because it was a secret that she gave away the note to be changed to buy silk, and my grandmother wasn't supposed to know.

My mother is much more frightened of my grandmother than I am of my mother. That's why she sometimes tells lies to my grandmother, but not to me, while I never have to lie to my mother. But if she kept on being strict with me, and scolding, well, then maybe I'd lie too.

My grandmother can't do anything to us, she has nothing but her sometimes stern words and the stern bonnet of her white hair. She never hits us. And often she's friendly and kind.

My mother couldn't stand it any more, and she told my grandmother all about the Bottom Dollar, and then my grandmother got angry with my mother, and with Hitler, and with the man who had skedaddled. They spent almost all the time talking about the man and the ten dollars, and I'm afraid I got a bit bored.

I played by the Mediterranean; the beach isn't sand, but beautiful white pebbles, as shiny white and smooth as the sun. The sun sends down swords from the sky, but it isn't warming. And the plants here are warlike plants. Giant cacti grow on the rocky cliffs, their prickly leaves are dangerous. You can kill someone with them if you hit them with them.

The leaves of the palm trees are sharp green swords. The oranges and lemons look like golden cannonballs. The whole town is like a fortress stuck up on rocks. Some rocks sprout out of the sea, where the bright little café is, where the waves boil white and foamy between. In the middle of it is a tiny wooden hut, which is the WC – there isn't one in the café itself. Until then I had always thought the most unpleasant WCs were in Poland.

Some cacti have single flame-red or violet blossoms in

between their grey-green spiny leaves. The leaves of olive trees are silvery metal plates. In amongst them are the crazy yellow flowers of mimosas, like luminous grapes – the polleny flowers reach across every path, and each individual blossom is a tiny feathery ball.

I collected an awful lot of white stones; they were so white they sometimes frightened me. I know the animals felt the same way about things. I never saw any birds flying. There were never any sea creatures washed up on the beach. I never saw any little fishes swimming in the sea; on all the blossoms I never saw a single butterfly.

The whole world was far too beautiful and big and poisonous, and I sometimes froze like the white stones. My mother and my grandmother both got ill, because they couldn't tolerate the climate. The sky was so far away, the sun was so far away, there were never any calming clouds; everything was so hot and icy, hard and smooth. Far out to sea we saw occasional battleships swimming by.

All the purpose in my grandmother's eyes was quenched when she left to go to Genoa and then to Switzerland and back to Germany. Her mouth was so feeble and withered she could hardly kiss us with it. Her tears were pale and yellow; before that she had always cried good healthy pink tears when she said goodbye to us. My mother could only cry when it was too late, and the train was already moving.

*

My mother and I got on a big shiny pink bus to Nice that barrelled along the edge of precipices, on a road that always looked too narrow for it. Giant rocks bore down on us from one side; they wanted to break loose and smash everything in their path. And on the other side there was a sheer drop down to the sea. I covered my mother's eyes because she couldn't stand the sight, yet she couldn't take her eyes off it.

The bus had a radio which sang songs, so we could have flown into the glittering blue sea on a song. Then we would have rested for all time on the seabed, charmed and trapped, because you know it's not possible to open car doors under water. I wasn't at all afraid, because the people on the bus were so merry that you could tell nothing bad would ever happen to them.

At the border, green Italian soldiers did their trick of collecting everyone's passports again, and disappearing with them. If borders weren't always dreadful places, this border might have been a jolly, bright one. Because there were jolly-looking stalls on the roadside, children were playing, flowers grew out of the cliffs, the radio in the bus was singing and fiddling as softly as the sea. From afar towns glittered at us that were already in France.

In front of us and behind us there were lots of private cars. Three men were arrested because they had money on them. And to think that we're always afraid we'll be arrested because we have none.

When we arrived in Nice, it was already dark. We

went straight to the hotel where my father had told us to go. It was bang in the middle of the town, on a big square. It had green and cream furniture, and very pretty notepaper. We were tired, and went straight to bed.

That night, the world started to scream. It screamed: our bed was full of screaming, the whole hotel was full of screaming, the screaming grew louder and louder, the whole world was screaming.

My mother and I sat bolt upright in bed. We forgot to breathe and we forgot to talk and we forgot to ask questions. When I thought I had been screamed to death, I fell asleep. But I woke up again, to my surprise, and it was morning. The world was quiet again.

A fat dark jolly woman brought us our breakfast and laughed. That was Suzanne from Savoy.

The world hadn't screamed at all; it had just been a show of a thousand cockerels in the square in front of the hotel. Each one had wanted to be louder than all the others. The demonstration went on for three days and three nights. The world was as noisy as if it was a slaughterhouse.

The Germans were just starting to help themselves to Austria, but in Nice it was Carnival. Carnival is a little bit like a war. You don't have the feeling that all the Carnival people like each other very much. Everything's called a battle as well: the battle of flowers, the battle of confetti.

Tightly pressed together, there was an endless procession of people walking down the Avenue de la

Victoire, and the stalls selling bags of coloured confetti went on for hour after hour. People were throwing the confetti in each other's faces as hard as they could, preferably so that it would hurt. They stuffed confetti down each other's necks, and the mush of confetti on the ground grew deeper all the time.

Once, my mother cried because our shoes were torn and we were no longer able to withstand the horrible Carnival smoke. We were wading through masses of confetti with other people, forming a kind of tired creeping human snake. I almost suffocated, because a sailor aimed a bouquet of mimosas and violets at me and caught my mother in the eye. That hurt her.

When at last we could take refuge in a restaurant, my mother ordered a peppermint tea. She took off my shoes and poured the confetti out of them. That didn't really help at all. I've still got confetti coming out of me. In the café, my mother wrote seven postcards to friends in Germany. Confetti will keep on pouring out of me – our hotel rooms are full of it.

Generally we couldn't get across the Avenue de la Victoire to get back to our hotel from the beach, because it was closed off for a procession. We saw a lot of the procession: giant colourful wagons with giant masked people.

Sometimes we sat by the sea on white chairs on the Promenade des Anglais. We saw lots of rich tanned beautiful people, and cars too, and very poor old men and women. The American women were mostly wearing flat straw hats that the locals made.

A tiny child in Nice costume was selling violets in the cafés, and always seemed to lose about half of them. The grown-up flower-sellers wore local costume too, and they looked beautiful and jolly, and the Americans and English sometimes had their pictures taken with them arm in arm in front of the Café Savoy. When you got close to the beach, there were very few French, and almost only Americans and English. (I only got to tell them apart much later.)

Again, my father kept us waiting for a long time, but eventually he came. My mother could no longer stand to see the wonderful shops selling langoustines and vegetables, and all for so little money. She wanted to cook, that was the thing she most wanted to do in the world, and she no longer talked about anything else. To distract her, my father took us to Menton and to Monte Carlo, where my mother and I saw a huge wonderful aquarium while my father lost a hundred francs in the casino, playing roulette.

I know how to play roulette too, and I've been to the casino once in Ostende and once in Nice. I don't enjoy it very much, though, and it costs a lot of money; I like slot machines much better. For roulette you have to buy little different-coloured tokens made of horn that look very pretty, and it's actually a bit of a waste laying them on different squares on the green baize table, just for men with long-handled rakes to come along and rake them all up. Sometimes you get given a few, but by the end they're all gone again.

One hot day, when the sun was stabbing not just at midday but all day long, we drove to Juan les Pins, to go swimming there, because that's the only place on the whole Côte d'Azur that has soft sand. Everywhere else there are just those white stones that look so pretty and that hurt your feet when you go in the water. The water looks like the cleanest water in the world, but if you get really close to it, you'll see it's not that clean after all.

Suzanne our chambermaid gave us a little bouquet of lacquered olive twigs to pin to us. I don't like to eat olives, but my father does. Suzanne liked my father a lot. She was always laughing with him; she seemed to laugh all day anyway, and only cry very briefly and unexpectedly, and not because anything sad had happened.

Suzanne didn't like my father to be bothered by his room neighbours. There was an old woman who squawked all day like a parrot, or like the exhibition of cockerels. But Suzanne made sure she moved out after three days – even though she'd planned to stay for three months.

Chambermaids have a lot of power, and Suzanne was especially good at exercising hers. When the old lady rang, Suzanne wouldn't go, but just unscrewed the signal-light on the bell-board, so that the hotel management wouldn't be able to complain. When the lady was asleep, Suzanne would go up and down outside the door with the vacuum cleaner, and sometimes bash it against the door. When the lady spilled coffee in her bed, Suzanne didn't give her any fresh sheets. She waited till the normal day for sheet-changing came round.

But if my father was having a bath, Suzanne very quickly made the room so that we could sit in it and be cosy. When the lady went out, Suzanne made all the other rooms first, so that the lady's room still wasn't made by the time she came back. There are really a hundred and one things a chambermaid can do to annoy a guest – who wouldn't even notice they were being annoyed deliberately.

People always tell my father their secrets. Suzanne said there are some chambermaids who steal, and what they usually do is this: they bury the guests' pyjamas or nightdresses so far down under the bedclothes when the guest is about to leave that the guest doesn't see them and generally forgets them, or else thinks they've been packed already. If the guest can be bothered to write a letter, they find the things and hand them over to the management honestly to have them forwarded to them.

Suzanne said she knew chambermaids who stole more than that. We don't really know very many who do, but once my mother complained that they always stole her best blouses and underthings. But then Suzanne said with a very serious face that there was absolutely no sense in stealing bad things if you were going to steal. And that's true. Firstly, there's no pleasure in having bad things, and if it gets out, you can find yourself in just as much trouble over a torn old blouse as over the finest new silk stockings.

There were lots of other German writers in Nice. They all said you couldn't live anywhere on as little money as you could in the South of France. My father mostly sat with the other writers in the big Café Monnot on the Place de la Victoire, and drank Mirabelle and sometimes Pale Ale. Or he sat on the Place Massena, where lots of sailors came and went from all over the world. He came to know a great many sailors, who generally drank more than the poets, and my father generally preferred them to the poets too.

My mother made friends with a writer's wife who had rented three furnished rooms with her husband, and did the cooking and lived on next to nothing. When my mother heard that, she could stand it no longer. Finally my father was forced to concede that if we were prudent we could easily live for half a year, whereas otherwise we would be in dire straits again in just four weeks. He agreed that we should settle down and be prudent and avoid dire straits.

My mother rented two rooms and a stove. I have never seen her so happy. We bought pots and pans in the bazaar and spoons and knives and forks, and some very cheap pretty cotton print for summer dresses, because it was getting very hot now. My mother was able to run up the dresses on the concierge's sewing machine.

The next day we cooked, and I helped. We had artichokes with vinaigrette, which my father loves, and calf's liver and cauliflower, and then we each had a slice of pineapple, and saved the rest for another time. Then my father got cheese as well, and a cup of coffee with cognac, and a copy of *Paris-Soir*, and he was allowed to crawl on to the sofa.

My father was very happy and he thanked my mother and said there was much to be said for having this sort of quiet life. He asked for an exact breakdown of what everything had cost.

The calf's liver was a little charred, but that was because the pan was still new and not properly seasoned yet. The next day we planned to have celeriac and Provençal tomatoes with garlic, and we were going to buy a pot with a pink geranium. And for that evening we invited all the poets, and my father had permission to bring along a couple of sailors as well.

In the afternoon I went for a walk with my mother to Saint Maurice and from there into the mountains, where there are roaring waterfalls and a little village is built on a rocky outcrop. On our way back we went through the Italian quarter, which is terribly dirty and noisy and rambleshack, and where you can buy things especially cheaply. On the mountain pastures we had picked an olive branch and some lovely colourful flowers.

At home my father was sitting restlessly on the sofa, and he clapped his hands and said: 'Children, children, life can be so wonderful sometimes, maybe everything will pan out now, and our fortunes are going to change. This afternoon I visited the American Consul and Thomas Cook. I have our American visa, and our steamer tickets. I wanted it to come as a surprise to you, darlings. I've got some wonderful letters from over there. It looks as though I'll make a deal with MGM, but of course so much depends on being on the spot, instead of doing everything through intermediaries. Of course we won't stay there; our home remains in Europe – that's where my heart is, and if everything goes pear-shaped, that's where I want to be. Our ship is leaving Rotterdam in five days' time. Before that we need to meet some people in Saint Raphaël and in Avignon. The town of the Popes, Annie, remember! Then one last stay in Paris. The day before yesterday I met this very nice silk manufacturer from Lyons. He's leaving today, and invited us all to go and stay with him in Lyons. But we won't manage that this time, and he's probably not about to give money to start a magazine either. But he collects works of art, and I know someone with a Botticelli that always strikes me as remarkably genuine-looking – I have the feeling you just need to scratch it, to find a real old Italian master underneath. Somehow the thing seems more than just a fake to me. Well, it's worth bearing in mind anyway.

'Annie, sweetheart, we're going to offer hospitality to my dear colleagues tonight. I finally decided not to ask the two sailors along; there's no knowing what they might do to your pretty flat if they get drunk, or maybe actually they'll feel a bit inhibited. You've managed to make everything so cosy here, Annie! I can understand the appeal of domesticity, only I've never liked flowers on my desk.

'Now instead of the sailors I've brought along a couple of bottles of old Napoleon, and a bottle of dry champagne for you, Annie. Do we have any glasses? No, of course not. And no waiter to hand either. I must say, those bell-boards are deuced useful things to have around! And you're going to cook us something wonderful, Annie – I really had no idea I was married to such a first-rate cook. What are we having today? My God, Annie! Do you see from my question what a starchy paterfamilias I've become already? Are you happy, Annie?'

'No,' said my mother quietly and tired-sounding.

'Now, Annie, you're not about to spoil one of the few happy evenings of my life, are you? Come and give me a kiss! And Kully, are you looking forward to America?'

'Will we take our pots and pans with us?' I asked.

'Dear me, no, Kully,' exclaimed my father and laughed. 'What would we be needing all that junk for over there?'

*

In the end it all happened very quickly. We went to Amsterdam in one fell swoop, because there was no time and no money to break the journey and go anywhere else.

We arrived in Amsterdam in the evening, and were met by Herr Krabbe. Before we had left the platform, my father relieved him of every penny that he had on his person. Unfortunately, Herr Krabbe never has enough, and he even said that my father's last book hadn't made any money, even though it was surely his best.

My mother was so tired she almost fell out of the train. All through the journey she was thinking of Nice, and the blue sky, and our little flat, the wonderful cheap groceries, and the cooking pots and the geranium we'd left behind. She hated America, and didn't want to go.

My mother was nauseous, which I sometimes get too, after being on a train for a long time. Once when I flew on a plane from Vienna to Prague on my own, I didn't feel sick at all. The only reason I had to vomit was because everyone else was all around me. We encountered some turbulence; sometimes you have a feeling like that in a lift.

My father took my mother to a hotel near the station, put her to bed and tucked her in. She didn't feel up to travelling on to Rotterdam. She was to rest for a few hours, because our ship wasn't leaving Rotterdam till midnight. She wasn't to worry about a thing. My father went on to Rotterdam with me and our luggage, because he was excited and wanted to put everything behind him, especially the formalities, which are always very trying. I wasn't the least bit tired, because I had slept all the way up on the train, in my mother's lap.

My father had instructed Herr Krabbe to wake my mother in time to get her to the ship. At that time, Herr Krabbe was still terribly nice, and always wanted to be helpful and obliging. He was someone you could depend on.

The night and the port of Rotterdam were a black building, lights flickering and nothing clear. Everything was humming and buzzing; I could no longer tell the people from the lights reflected in the black water – none of it looked like the sea, but none of it looked like people either.

The ship was a castle with red carpets and servants. I didn't realize till much later that it was a ship. I had been on it for a long time without knowing I was. I kept on walking all over the ship, thinking it was a sort of overture to the real ship. I was laid out on a bed in a little room.

A woman like a nurse promised me my father would come soon with my mother. You couldn't see out of the window in the little room, but there was a little square of patterned tinted glass somewhere. Laughter and noise ran down the long corridor outside my room, and I could hear music far away.

When I woke up, my bed was shaking quietly and insistently, and there was a dull stamping sound coming from way down below me. On the bed opposite I saw my father with wild-looking hair. The ship was going. My mother hadn't come.

Later on we heard that Herr Krabbe had gone to the hotel, and had tried to get my mother woken up by phone. But out of ignorance and stupidity the staff of the hotel said my mother had already left. When my mother woke up, there was just enough time to get to the ship in Rotterdam. But she didn't have a penny to get to Rotterdam, and Herr Krabbe couldn't be found anywhere. All the time, my father supposed my mother was on the ship, and in the cabin with me.

First, my father ran with me to the ship's telegraphist. We wired Herr Krabbe to say that she should fly to Boulogne or Cherbourg, where our ship was stopping. Then we had a terrible panic that something had happened to my mother, and we sent another wire. My father didn't get undressed; all night he didn't sleep, while I kept on waking up.

Early in the morning, we got a telegram from Herr Krabbe saying my mother was still alive and healthy. But she couldn't fly to Boulogne, because my father had her passport with him. We had completely forgotten about that.

I really wanted to get out in Boulogne, but we didn't have any money for that. All we could do was send my mother the passport from Boulogne, and get her to take the next ship after us. But even that couldn't be done easily, because the ships didn't go every day. It had to be a ship of the same company and in the same price range. Because there are also much more expensive ships, which are bigger and sail faster.

Our ship was very big too. A couple of times I walked from one end of it to the other. But once we were in the middle of the ocean, it didn't feel so big to me any more. I had a clear sense that it was a ship, and it seemed to get smaller with each passing day. A real ship, on the other hand, would have to be smaller still, so that you could reach out and touch the water, and feel you really were sailing.

I did once go sailing in Denmark, and that's why I was hardly afraid at all now. In fact, I wasn't ever really afraid; just on the third day I badly wanted to get off. I had to keep thinking of my mother, who was never alone in her life, only sometimes without my father. But now she didn't even have me to protect her. I could picture her crying, and doing unbalanced things.

Who will be sleeping with her? She's always so afraid at night; she needs to have somebody with her at night, definitely. My father's good at sleeping by himself, but I don't like it much myself. Even if you're fast asleep, it's good to have the feeling that there's someone sleeping lovingly near you. I hope my mother doesn't have to sleep all by herself, and I hope she finds some kind creature that doesn't bite her or thrash around in its sleep.

I spoke to my father about it, and suggested he wire Herr Krabbe and get him to sleep with her, but my father refused point-blank to do that, and it wasn't even a question of money for the telegram either; he even wired the lady with the bird's nest, and asked her to keep an eye on my mother. But my mother won't want to sleep with the bird's nest, because she doesn't smell nice, and she snores so foully that you're amazed at how a human being who's fairly quiet in the daytime can make such a racket at night. We got some sense of what it was like when she had an afternoon nap for an hour or so on the sofa in our hotel in Ostende.

There's never any point in telling people that they snore like rattlesnakes or like trumpets with sore throats – they never know what they do when they're asleep, and they never believe you when you tell them.

I thought Herr Krabbe was much more appropriate to take over sleeping duties with my mother, but unfortunately it seems his nights are already spoken for. That's why he can't help us out this time. My mother ought to get hold of a little Dutch child from somewhere, but I'm afraid I don't know of a suitable one.

We're travelling first class on the ship, because that way they'll let us out on land more readily, but also because an American friend of my father's lent him some travelling money.

The wind and the waves are both capable of moving our gigantic ship, and if my bed didn't have rails I could hold on to, I would fall out of bed at night sometimes. When you want to go down to the dining room, the steps seem to move – it's all as exciting as a funfair.

The doors that open out on to the deck and the fresh air are held shut so tight by the wind and rain that I can't open them by myself. A fat friendly sailor in a white suit always helps me. At first I took him for the captain, but his name is Deck Steward. Later on, I did meet the captain with my father, and tried hard to be nice to him. I addressed him as 'Mr Deck Steward'. But my father said that was wrong, and a captain was more important. He's something like the king of a ship. Everything goes by the number of golden rings that seamen have sewn on to the sleeves of their navy blue jackets.

The captain and the chief officer are supposed to steer the ship, but usually they let it go by itself, because they're too busy attending to the travelling ladies, dancing with them and taking them on tours of the ship. I expect those ladies have to pay a higher price for the privilege. Only when there's fog, and a foghorn toots, do the officers get all excited and run off.

A lot of passengers got seasick and didn't want to eat any more, or even go down to the dining room, because that's where the floor shook the most. On such a ship, you're given the most wonderful things to eat, and you can have as much as you want. I ate so much, my belly got to be as round as a ball. My father said he felt embarrassed to be arriving in New York with such a fat emigrant child as me.

My father didn't get sick, but he didn't want to eat either. He was really odd altogether, more than I've ever known him to be. On the fifth day, he suddenly couldn't stand to be on the ship any more. He didn't want to speak to anyone, he hated all the people. He hated the dining room with the beautiful flowers on the tables, and the naked ladies in their evening dresses. He didn't want to lie down on a deckchair or play deck quoits, even though on the ship all the adults were running and leaping about like children who weren't even as old as me.

He didn't even want to go to the cinema with me, so I went once by myself. It was jolly boring, I can tell you, watching adults kissing the whole time. Later, I met some sailors who spoke English, but unfortunately they didn't always have time for me.

Once or twice, I secretly climbed down to the third-class section. There I met three children from Berlin, who were emigrating to America with their parents for good. They were pretty sad, and didn't talk much. One time an older boy said to me: 'You're not a proper emigrant, you're not even Jewish, you're luxury emigrants.'

One evening I stood on the middle deck all alone, and thought of my mother. I so badly wanted to send her some lovely food. On the ship you got everything for nothing. I could have ordered fifty roast beefs and chickens and strawberries and secretly packed everything up and sent it off. But how? Just make up a parcel, write the address and toss it into the sea? Would that ever get there? But telegrams do.

Stormy waves came as high as the deck, and the spray wet my feet. If you're in the middle of the ocean, the sky gets to be as tight as a cheese cloche. You can't see nearly as far as you'd like to.

My father was almost always lying silently and grumpily on the bed in his cabin. Sometimes he would be up in the smoking saloon, drinking whiskey, which cost extra. Apart from that we had nothing to worry about all the time we were on the ship; we had never known such ease. My mother would certainly have been happy there.

For the whole crossing, my father was grumpy. He didn't want to be bothered with me. One time an English-woman wanted me to play bridge with her, but I didn't know how, and I didn't feel like learning either. Then she said I ought to cheer my father up, so that he didn't drink so much whiskey and rum. But if you do that, you can really put someone on edge who doesn't want to be cheered up.

I don't like playing cards, I prefer dice. Sometimes I played dice with the ship's doctor, who didn't have anything better to do, because the passengers could be seasick without his help, and there weren't any other sicknesses going.

I didn't know any more whether we'd been sailing for a hundred days or just a week. I couldn't imagine ever arriving anywhere. In some mysterious way, the ship even managed to print a newspaper, and I read in it that it was May, when my mother has her birthday.

It's not unusual for my mother and me to not know what month we're in, because the seasons are different in all the countries. When we left Nice, it was summer – and a day later it was rain and winter and Amsterdam.

We don't have any other ways of clinging on to the time either. Sometimes we just find out by chance that it's Sunday or Christmas or All Souls. Once we nearly mistook Easter for Whitsun. We often lose track of how long we've been gone from Germany, and what year it is. One day we'll forget our birthdays, and then we won't know how old we are.

Often we have no idea how long we've spent in a place. There's only one unpleasant way of finding out, which is via the hotel bill. Then it always turns out we've been there much longer than we thought.

On the ship there was no time at all, and we were all alone in the world. Only once, in fog, we heard the tooting of another ship, and we tooted back.

One day the air felt hot and clammy, and the steward-ess told me we were crossing the Golf Stream. I've seen lots of golf courses, especially in England, where the whole country consists of little else. So I would have loved to see a Golf Stream, especially because it made the air and the ship so hot. But I couldn't see it anywhere, and I didn't feel like asking anyone either, because they mostly just laughed. Not that they managed to explain it to me either. You really have to find out for yourself how everything in the world is arranged. I've managed to find out quite a lot of things already.

All at once, the sea got very busy. Other ships came sailing towards us from miles away, seagulls fluttered up, and three times big fishes jumped right out of the water. My father cheered up a bit, the passengers were almost cured of their seasickness and laughed excitedly. Suddenly the dining room was full of people I'd never seen before, and the deck as well. What was with them all?

My father went downstairs with me to eat. The music was livelier, the conversation more animated. Lots of people who hadn't spoken to each other before quickly made friends, and then forgot each other again. I had known them all along anyway. My father laughed when I told him about that, and ate a capon, and said: 'Tomorrow we'll be in New York.' In the evening he wanted to go for a walk with me all over the whole ship, from the topmost deck down to the very lowest.

Everyone was talking about packing, and I packed my father's suitcase, just as I had learned to do from my mother. I didn't need to pack my own case, because I'd never unpacked it. I'd kept the same dress on all through.

It was a bit dirty. Also I hadn't combed my hair much, and I hadn't put on a nightie to go to bed, and sometimes I hadn't said my prayers. I hadn't had to wash either.

One night I had to cry because I thought of my mother. I wrote to her for forgiveness, and promised I would have a bath for a whole hour to make up. I did, too. Sometimes I liked it very much on the ship.

The next morning, my father was friends with practically everyone on board. We stood on deck and saw cheerful green hills with red houses; the sea got narrower till it was like navigating in a river. We saw a big monument in the water, called something like Freedom Statue, but really it was just of a fat jolly-looking woman. Houses like big toyboxes came nearer, and a little boat made fast to our ship and unloaded some men with briefcases that were half detectives, half officials. Men like that are always a pain because their job is checking up on people and passports.

We landed in Hoboken, which is a sort of outskirt of New York. We distributed our money to the stewards and the musicians till we didn't have any left for ourselves. The barman brought my father a big glass of sherry down to his cabin, where he was sitting with a whole lot of newspapermen. My father's American publishers had let them know we were coming.

They were sitting on our cases and on our beds, but it wasn't truly my bed. I had slept alone all the way across. Never in my life did I have to sleep on my own for so long, and I told the newspaper people, because they wanted to hear what we had to say, and my father doesn't like talking so much in the morning. He doesn't like being asked things at any time really.

It was hard to understand what the men were saying. They didn't speak English like in England; they chewed the words in their mouths and didn't let them out properly because they kept grinning through their teeth. But before long I could understand them all right. They had very friendly eyes, and they were terribly nice really, and I'm sure they would have played with me too, if they didn't have to ask my father so many questions.

Of course I was cautious, though, because I knew from the newspapers that plenty of children are stolen in America, especially rich children. That's why I told them to put in their newspapers that my father is completely broke, and we've got absolutely no money at all. My father was furious about that, because no one was meant to know, but I had to be mindful of the danger. I was pleased that the journalists wrote down what I told them.

'How do you like America?' they asked. I said straight away that I liked it fine, because I felt really pleased that we'd finally arrived. The American buildings and seagulls had looked very nice too from the ship.

My father growled something in English that no one understood. They fired lots and lots of questions at him. In the end he got impatient, and started to glower at them. I'm familiar with that; it means it's time to leave him in peace. Now he wanted to finally set eyes on America and a hotel room. He couldn't get any more sherry either, because we had absolutely no money.

'What's your favourite book?' the men asked him.

'A cheque book.'

'What's your favourite sport?'

'Running amok,' said my father, and at that he really did run away.

In our last few days in Europe we had talked about America all the time and looked at photos of it, but in fact I thought it looked completely different from the way we'd pictured it. Europe is actually much more American, because things there are much more hectic.

When the customs official unpacked our suitcases in Hoboken, he found a book of my father's, and being a keen reader, he settled down on the floor and started reading it. My father gave him the book, because we didn't want to wait for him to finish it.

That evening I went to a Communist meeting, where I got lost.

My father's friends hadn't met us off the boat, so, without any money, we had to drive to a hotel near Broadway, which is my favourite street in the world. That's because, right on Broadway itself, there's an enormous building that has hundreds of pinball machines; you can play with one for just one cent. You can let balls roll down so that they set off little electric lamps or illuminated scenes. And outside in the window there are loads of little tortoises, with red- and blue- and green-lacquered shells and flowers painted on them.

It never occurred to me that you can produce such magnificence with tortoises, and apparently it doesn't do them any harm either. I wrote to tell my mother about it right away, because my tortoises had stayed behind with her, but she's not to dye them; I want to do it myself when I go back. Because my poor mother isn't now coming to join us in America, as she had to sell her ticket to live off the money.

Well, on my very first evening, I got lost in a Communist meeting, but it wasn't so bad, and later I got to know my way around New York better than in most other cities. We were staying in a very large and interesting hotel with a swimming pool and a drugstore in the basement – a drugstore is a shop where you can sit and drink all kinds of iced drinks and at the very same time buy all sorts of stuff. Our room had a radio in it and a refrigerator and a buzzing air-conditioner.

My father was on the telephone for hours, and at the end of that he practically collapsed. First, the operator wouldn't understand the number he wanted, and later on the people themselves didn't understand him. He had made ten appointments, and he wasn't sure where or when any of them was supposed to be. America was too bewildering for him.

He fell asleep in his clothes on the bed, I fell asleep in

the chair – it was pretty hot. We were both woken up by a fat friendly man unpacking suitcases and setting up lights. He was a photographer, and he was supposed to take pictures of us for a magazine.

Those hideous bright lamps were the reason it was discovered that I hadn't really washed for a long time. We had a bathroom handy, and I was packed off there right away. I would rather have gone downstairs to the swimming pool. The dirt wasn't really my fault; it was mainly because at the end of our time on the boat I'd made friends with a couple of stokers.

My father was able to order some whiskey to our room, and then he got talking to the photographer. They didn't really understand what each other was saying, but they got on really well together even so. They would each take a sip of whiskey at the same moment, and smile at each other. When one of them stopped speaking, the other would begin. Finally the photographer agreed to telephone for my father. He straightened out one appointment, and said lots of things very fast.

I had to write everything down, and later I was told I had written it down all wrong. My father went out and met people, but they weren't the ones he was supposed to try and meet. Among others he met a German waiter who helped him rent an old car, and in a French restaurant he almost married the cook.

I already understood from Herr Krabbe that in America I would have to watch my father like a hawk, to make sure he doesn't suddenly get married, because in America you can get married just like that, and if a man was in a hurry he could easily get married five times in a single day, or even more. Even though it's so easy, it's illegal, and in fact it's severely punishable. It seems to me it would be better if illegal things were difficult, especially for foreigners who aren't sure what's permitted and what isn't.

In Italy we met a man who had to pay a two hundred lire fine for kissing a famous girl on the street. After that I was always afraid when my grandmother wanted to kiss me in public somewhere. It made her cross, and she called me standoffish, but two hundred lire was a lot of money for us just then.

The car my father rented in America was almost the end for us, because he drove it beautifully but always in some unlawful way.

On that first evening, my father had no use for me. But I didn't feel like sleeping, so I was left in the hands of the photographer. My father preferred me not to be left on my own, because he had heard that a gangster had been shot in the room above us. Probably it was one who had been stealing children. But I wasn't scared any more, not since I'd seen America and the Americans for myself.

The photographer had to take pictures of a Communist meeting, and he took me with him. First he went looking through my suitcase for an intact pair of socks. When he couldn't find any, I was allowed to take off my holey ones and not wear any. That's what I prefer anyway. Men are always much nicer and more sensible about these things than women anyway. I prefer their company too; old ladies I always find are particularly dangerous to children.

In America I met women who wanted me to look like Shirley Temple, and always have clean fingernails. But it's not possible for me to look as nice as little girls in films. And my nails get dirty absolutely by themselves. I really don't get them like that on purpose or because I'm naughty.

Before we went out, I unpacked my father's suits and hung them up in the wardrobe because that's what my mother always does. The photographer helped me, and it was he who found the three mutton chops and the piece of liver that I'd completely forgotten about.

I had collected the mutton chops and the liver on the ship, and secretly packed them in the suitcase so that I could send them to my mother later from New York. Both of those things are particular favourites of hers. But the meat didn't look so nice any more, and it didn't smell at all nice either. The photographer threw the whole lot out of the window. It was just as well too, I think. My father's favourite pale trousers had a stain, but thank God it was over the b*m. It's always other people who see stains like that, you never see them yourself, and so there's really no need for you to feel annoyed or ashamed.

The photographer went down in the lift with me, rushing through thousands of storeys – America's so nice like that. Perhaps the mutton chops hadn't yet hit the ground, that's how high up we were staying.

Before the meeting we stopped at a stand where I sat on a high stool in front of a bar, and drank fresh pineapple juice, and ate as much coloured ice as I wanted. I could have done that on the ship as well, but unfortunately I didn't get to hear about it till it was too late.

Then we drove in a car to Central Park. Central Park is amazing and very big, you're allowed to run on the grass and feed little grey squirrels. But that evening the squirrels were already tucked up in bed in their tall dark trees. I watched the buildings rise like giant castles into the sky, which was deep dark blue behind a veil of hot pink light. So much light was bubbling up out of the skyscrapers that I felt like picking up an empty mineral water bottle and filling it up with the frothy light to give my mother in Amsterdam later.

The Communist meeting was in a hall that was as big as a hundred theatres put together. Sometimes it was boring, and sometimes as rowdy as Carnival. Streamers were thrown, people sat in smoke and dust. There were Negroes there as well, I even got to sit next to one. He gave me a stick of chewing gum.

A stage was covered with flags, flags soared up into the smoky air. Sometimes a man got to speak, sometimes a woman – their voices came shouting through big funnels. People clapped and shouted, photographers scuttled this way and that, and sometimes there were flashes of brilliant white light.

Once I was allowed to go outside with the photographer and eat hot dogs at a bar and drink a cup of coffee, then after that I got tired. I went out to get some air. There were lots of policemen standing around.

I went for a walk, and because it was dark I suddenly lost my bearings. I spent a long time looking for the Communist meeting, and then I looked for our hotel, and I couldn't find that either. I was so tired I forgot to take the chewing gum out of my mouth. I think chewing was making me even more tired.

I didn't cry, and I wasn't afraid either. Sometimes I had the feeling I was still on the ship, which was rocking and stamping under me. The air smelled of the sea. It was a warm May evening. I wanted to think of gardens with lilac and go to sleep in them, only you don't get lilac flowering by the sea.

My mother always wanted to see the lilac in her birthday month of May. She told me about little red villages that were buried under white and purple flowering lilac bushes. Every individual bloom kissed you with its scent, and numbed you and made you good and made you want to kiss other people. Pink hawthorn bushes surrounded the villages like cheerful red and green bungalow roofs. The meadows had soft green hair garlanded with golden buttercups. Glittering streams whispered the secrets of the meadows, and the air was so mild it turned the whole night into a downy bed. So my mother told me. Now when will I see it?

I crossed a large and handsome stone street. The houses were getting taller and taller, and looked as though giant children had been playing a game with giant building blocks, and as if all the buildings would fall down if one more block was put on top of them.

I often played like that myself earlier, when I used to have three sets of building blocks. I always enjoyed building. But once everything had fallen down, I had to tidy it all away. I would never be able to tidy New York away if it collapsed, I was already far too tired.

I saw some wonderful flower shops, and some of the flowers looked almost like lilacs – maybe they were lilacs. Unfortunately I couldn't smell them through the plate-glass windows. But women walked past me with wafts of scent, and I quickly did some magic: I looked at all the lilac-like flowers in the shop window and at the same time I smelled what the women wafted at me – and suddenly I had lilac and May and my mother. I kissed the window, and so I kissed her.

As I did, I remembered the nasty chewing gum that was still in my mouth. I took it out and stuck it on the window. Unfortunately I couldn't remember where I was staying, I barely knew my name. That's why I couldn't stop a car and ask the driver to take me home. I had done that kind of thing before.

I wanted to be a bird made out of lilac, and I became one and fluttered between the giant stone houses. My feathers were lilac, and I sang and twittered little birdsongs. It was so pretty to listen to, I sang louder and louder. All at once a policeman grabbed me. He completely failed to understand that I was a fluttering songbird. He didn't even like my singing. But it hadn't been me singing; it was the lilac bird singing and wafting scent.

I really wasn't myself at the moment the policeman picked me up, but later on I was able to describe my father and our hotel to him. He led me by the hand, and was quite nice to me. As we happened to be passing it, he pointed out the Empire State Building to me, which is the tallest building in New York. We stood at the foot of it, and looked up, and I couldn't even see the top. Afterwards I went up there once, and then I could see everything. Now I understand why people are always talking about 'making it to the top' – you can see so much more from up there.

And the policeman duly asked me: 'How do you like America?'

'Yes,' I said, and before I fell asleep, he was carrying me again. And he kindly warned me not to sing again while I was in New York.

I could explain to him that I wasn't singing for money, and that it wasn't my fault that it sounded so horrible. But how could I explain to him that someone other than myself had been doing the singing? Why did I like it so much? And why did everyone else think it was horrible? Now I'm never going to sing again.

I was dropped off in the hotel – my father wasn't back yet. I was put in the lift, and all the men took off their hats for me. The hotel management let me into our room with a little star-shaped key. On the bed, which was still its daytime-sofa self, were my torn socks – I lay down on them and fell asleep, because the holey socks were proof that this was where I belonged.

I didn't see much of my father in New York. He was running around all over the place, much more than any American. He was trying to pull off deals that wouldn't be pulled off. Once, he was paid some money by a little man called Mr Lief, who was an agent.

But what good was that? My father gave me his cents, so I could play on the slot machines, on those thousands and thousands of amazing slot machines that America has. And the dollars my father gave to poor emigrants, some of whom were so poor that they even had a use for ten dollars.

I sometimes think my father wouldn't be rich even if he was a millionaire, but then again he isn't poor even when he hasn't got a cent to his name. He once said: money runs away from young men, pretty women run away from old men, and some men live to experience both – in which case either they kill themselves, or they become wise and happy. What they're left with are children and dogs.

In his old car, my father drove himself and me through America. In America only rich people take trains, the poor drive everywhere.

There were no deals to be made in New York, and we were in desperate difficulties. The American publisher took us to lunch once at the Rockefeller Center, and then he lost interest in us and went away. The other people we could have turned to went fishing.

My father would greet each day by vomiting in the sink; he usually does that when times are especially exciting. When it's like that, I know better than to ask any questions.

Thank God my father remembered a boyhood friend of his who had emigrated. That is, he'd never really liked him when he was a boy, because he was so stupid. But apparently the stupidity has abated, slightly.

This man lived in Virginia, a long way away, where he owns a gentlemen's outfitters, which is like a clothes shop, only better. He was making a lot of money. My father called him at the hotel's expense. The telephone call gave the man the impression that we were hugely wealthy, and he invited us to his cottage in Virginia Beach.

I cried because I had no idea how we were going to get back to Europe and my mother. In her letters she was mentioning the war again. In Virginia they mentioned the war a lot too, but it wasn't one that might be coming, but one they'd had fifty or a hundred or two hundred years before, called the Civil War.

They didn't have too much idea about Europe. They thought things like Denmark was a French port, and Marseilles a Spanish river. But then we hardly know anything about America. I went up to the top of the Empire State Building once, and looked over the vast expanse of New York as far as the sea. And I thought that was it, that was all of America. But really it was just beginning.

My father told his boyhood friend something about money transfers from Europe being late. The only currency for which the Americans don't have contempt are English pounds. And that's why my father was careful to mention them specifically. After that his boyhood friend sent him some dollars. That was so we could pay for the hotel.

We couldn't afford the train, but then we had our old car. By the time we left New York, we'd been fined seven times, and had run over someone's soda fountain. My father had had enough of the police, and I think the police had had enough of him too. As soon as we were out of the city, we were unmolested.

We had our boat tickets back to Europe, but our ship wasn't due to leave for another three weeks, and my father wanted to see his publisher again, and wait for the decision on a film script first. So we needed somewhere to stay till then. We drove for three days. At night we slept either in the car, or in the open air; once was by the banks of the Delaware, which is so huge I don't think it should qualify as a river at all.

After that, we saw more rivers as big, including some with beautiful, wild, floating islands in them. Everything in America is so gigantically huge that the whole of Europe felt to me like my doll's kitchen. You don't notice the size of the houses so much, because they're built miles away from each other, surrounded by gardens and parks, and anyway the whole country is so enormous.

Everything is there. The rivers are as wide as seas, the forests are as wild and endless as the forests in Indian stories, and the highways go on for ever. The heat is so baking hot, your feet burn through the thin soles of your shoes. If it rains, a waterfall comes down from the sky, the cars turn into motorboats, and you can happily drown in the street. One time in Norfolk, Virginia, I swam from one side of the road to the other, with three Negro children.

When I was in Ostende, I found a shell as big as a matchbox, and kept it because I thought it was such a freak. On the beach in Virginia I found shells as big as my father's shoes. I was terribly excited. At first I couldn't believe it, and thought the Americans must have manufactured those giant shells and left them for publicity. But they were real seashells all right. By the way, there are absolutely no shells in Nice and in Bordighera. Only those white stones.

If we had driven like the wind, we could have got to my father's boyhood friend in Virginia Beach in a single day. We did drive like the wind, actually, only a lot of the time we were going the wrong way. Sometimes the car just stopped, because there was something wrong with it. Then we couldn't do anything, but just sat there and waited for another car to come and help.

My father doesn't have the first idea of how a car works. He can't learn either, he can't even take apart and fix a fountain pen. Only clocks he loves repairing. He hurls himself at any clock within reach, even though my mother has officially banned him. His repairs have caused a lot of irritation and expense, because afterwards the clocks are always so well and truly broken that no one can fix them.

Sometimes we puttered along from gas station to gas station. People were always terribly nice to us, only neither of us wanted to drink the American national beverage, which is a sort of brown fizzy lemonade that tastes of liquid mothballs. Americans drink it nonstop. In fact my father doesn't like lemonade, period, and that's what made it difficult for him in Virginia.

Once we'd rendezvoused with Boyhood Friend in Norfolk and driven him to Virginia Beach, we went to a restaurant with him, feeling tired but happy. We felt we were safe at last.

We were so pleased to have found the man. We almost loved him because we'd have been lost without him, and because it was really him. That's why we hardly listened to what he was saying, and didn't check to see what he looked like. If we hadn't felt so happy, we might have just gone to sleep.

We'd raced all over America for three days, and felt we no longer had any hope of finding New York or Europe or Virginia and Boyhood Friend again. I didn't even care that he had long hairs growing out of his nose, and that he was like a little worm that crept along instead of walking.

He was telling us he had won a prestigious position among real Americans. We didn't even listen to him. We kissed him. I did too. At the same time my father wanted to kiss the waitress out of sheer delight, and order a round of whiskeys to have a cosy chat and celebrate their seeing each other again after so many years, and meanwhile I was to eat – never mind what, just eat.

It was true, we hadn't eaten or drunk anything for days, and my father got so thirsty sometimes he wished he could drink the last of our petrol from the tank.

And then everything turned out to be impossible. First, my father was prevented from kissing the waitress. Then Boyhood Friend told him he couldn't get whiskey because the serving of alcoholic beverages was illegal in the state of Virginia.

'I see,' said my father, and grew pale, 'so that's what I get in the Land of the Free, that's where you invited me to!' After that, he didn't want to speak any more.

My father calmed down a little when Boyhood Friend told him you could get wine and beer in some joints on Virginia Beach – Californian wine. My father tried some of that Californian wine later, and hated it so much, he said he'd rather drink hair oil. But then every place also has somewhere where they sell alcohol, called an ABC.♪¼ And my father was consoled when he heard that we'd be staying very near one of those in Virginia Beach.

My father told Boyhood Friend about the cocktails in New York; he had sampled every single one, and that had aged him by years, and comprehensively poisoned his system: 'Every morning I fought for my life in the bathroom. And the little girl can confirm that.'

Then Boyhood Friend wanted to reminisce with my father about their shared boyhood – only for them each to tell completely different stories, whereupon it emerged that they had got each other mixed up, and they hadn't gone to the same school at all, and in fact had never met before. My father cried that he was now twice as glad to meet Boyhood Friend, and he laughed and shouted excitedly. In time, he even managed to produce a kind of retrospective association with Boyhood Friend. After a while, they both thought they had been boyhood friends after all.

Boyhood Friend told us there was a German recording

---

* Perversely named retail outlet for the Department of Alcoholic Beverage Control. (Trans.)

in this restaurant that he often asked to hear. He suggested my father listen to that, in lieu of whiskey.

I ate a big plate of rice with shrimp, which are a kind of pink prawns, though they don't taste of fish, they taste of nothing at all. If you put some in tomato sauce and shredded lettuce, you get a prawn cocktail, which my father ordered because of the name, but that turned out to be very unsatisfactory. He was feeling pretty tired and drained, but he kept trying to gee up Boyhood Friend, who didn't even know yet that we had no money and weren't going to get any from Europe.

Boyhood Friend was complaining about business being bad. My father said he couldn't imagine such a thing in America, and was very supportive. Boyhood Friend envied my father for having turned into such a famous writer, and said he must have loads of money, and had a fascinating life. He was proud of my father, and had told all his friends about him coming, and even read one of his books. The book turned out not to be one by my father at all.

Then the gramophone record played, and Boyhood Friend swayed his head around and got rheumy eyes. A man was gently and sadly singing: 'When I got home – there she was, the old sweetheart!'

At first my father looked a bit surprised, but then he said: 'Nice, very nice. That's a type of nostalgia I can understand, I myself can remember a female lavatory attendant . . .'

'Listen to it all,' said Boyhood Friend. And the gramophone voice went on sorrowfully: 'And mother smiled at my old sweetheart . . .' After that everything was quiet.

'Bewildering,' said my father, 'such a mixture of sentimentality and plain speaking. Extraordinary, old boy, I wouldn't have expected such a thing in America – maybe it's only possible in the South. Where was the record produced? Quite remarkable, a mother like that, when I think of my own – rather charming, though, of such a woman to smile at an old tart.'

'What are you talking about?' asked Boyhood Friend. 'For Christ's sake, not so loud! I know the people at the next table, and they're here with their wives. I know one of them speaks German.'

'Really very interesting,' said my father. 'There's always more to learn, every country seems to harbour its own contradictions. All I ask of you is that you continue to point them out to me, my man. So, here in this respectable restaurant, they're quite openly singing a song about an old tart, but to speak on such a subject is not permissible.'

'What song are you talking about?'

'Why, the one you just had played.'

'What, the one about the sweetheart?'

'Sweetheart?' said my father. 'Ah, a little mishearing, I must be exhausted. What word did you think the man sang, Kully?'

'Tart.'

'You see, old man – it's all right, the girl has no idea what's meant, anyway she's dead on her feet. Shall we head off, old man, and see what sort of billet you've got in mind for us? I think it's better, by the way, if you take care of our bills. I don't think I've got the hang of this foreign money yet, and I don't know how they tip here. But you mentioned an ABC store a while ago. I'd be keenly interested to see that – fascinating to me as a writer, of course. We might stop off on the way, what'd you say?'

Virginia Beach was beautiful, the beach itself was endlessly long and wide. There were little green lawns between the pretty little houses. We were staying in a cottage at the edge of a forest, which was also endlessly long and wide.

All the people were happy and tanned and ran around in just their swimming costumes. It got so hot, you almost couldn't bear to move. Even my father lay there stiffly and silently for hours on end in the water next to Boyhood Friend.

But there was some astonishing wildlife on the beach too. Strange little black eyes popped out of holes in the sand. The beast they belonged to came out after them and whisked across the beach on long legs. Then it vanished into another hole, and I was never able to capture one. They look like a cross between giant spiders and crabs.

I would have liked to watch the animals digging their holes and seen whether they do it from inside or from outside. My father didn't like the creatures. He was suspicious of them, and thought they only craftily used holes that other animals had dug.

Once I saw a rattlesnake in the forest, but I wasn't allowed to go near it. I'm interested in snakes. The snake is a criminal, you see, and, as it says in the Bible, it was always up to mischief. By way of punishment it was told it had to creep on its belly all the days of its life. But I don't think it had legs up to that point either. I've seen loads of pictures of Adam and Eve and the serpent, as they sometimes call it. Every snake I've seen looks identical before and after, and I've yet to see a single one that could run or fly.

Once I saw a big field full of flowering white camellias. The blossoms were bedded like chilly snow-white stars against the dark green leaves; they were the whitest flowers I've ever seen. In Europe they cost a fortune, and here they just come out of the ground for nothing. There were also amazing water lilies that kids sold or gave away and trampled on.

Great and small tortoises swam in streams in the forest or pottered around on land. By the end I had seventeen and they stank up the cottage quite a bit. I observed exactly how much they had to eat, and I was never able to understand that ten times more stuff came out of them than had gone into them by way of food and water. It was as if it secretly multiplied in their stomachs.

Boyhood Friend partly got used to us, partly he was fed up with us because he wanted to get married. As long as we were in the cottage, there was nowhere for him to keep a woman.

If my mother had been able to see the house, she would have fainted with happiness. And all the houses were as nice as that one, especially the ones with electric refrigerators in their kitchens, where you could make ice all day long.

Every morning Toxy came, who was a lovely Negro girl, and we used to tidy up the house together and cook. Sometimes Toxy would forget to come, or else she'd got hold of some money and then she didn't bother. Then things would get a bit untidy in the house, and Boyhood Friend was embarrassed if visitors came. He had his clothes store in Norfolk, and he drove there every morning and came back every night. It was half an hour's drive. Just like everyone in Holland and Denmark has bicycles, everyone in America has cars; it's nothing special at all. But also there are some people who are dirt poor, and they have absolutely nothing.

My father was completely fed up with the heat and beach life. He didn't know what to do all day with no money, he couldn't sit in a bar or restaurant. But he made friends with a salesman in the ABC store, who would sometimes sell him a bottle of gin on credit.

In the evenings he had to sit out on the veranda for hours with Boyhood Friend, while glow-worms buzzed around, even though he had no idea what to talk about with him. Most interesting to him were the cheery Negroes, who shined people's shoes on the sidewalk. He often hung around with them in the daytime.

The first time I saw a Negro, in Belgium, I trailed around after him for hours. In America I saw so many of them, I didn't even stare at them any more. But to begin with I thought they were terribly exciting, and I wished I could touch them all. I hadn't known that there were children who were already Negroes.

We drove through lots of towns, most of them were as beautiful as tourist towns in Germany and Austria, but much bigger. All the towns had coloured quarters, where the Negroes could live amongst themselves.

They were always spilling out on to the street; I've never known them to stay in their own houses. They make an awful lot of noise. When they hear music play, they start dancing right away, wherever they are, on the street, in a store, in a drugstore. In the evenings, they're all drunk, and worst of all on Sundays. If they own cars, they have wrecks on Sunday nights, because they drive around like mad and crash into each other.

One time I was in a Negro house in Norfolk. That was terrible.

The jolly Negro shoe-shine man was very sad one day,

because his wife had died. She had to be buried by a Negro firm of undertakers. The shoe-shine man didn't have enough money to pay for the funeral, because he had lent some to his brother, who could only repay him in four days' time.

My father couldn't endure so much unhappiness, and so he lent the Negro the money which he'd just been lent himself, by Boyhood Friend. That way, the wife did get to be buried after all.

At the end of four days, we had to go to Norfolk, because we had an invitation. On our way, we passed the Negro walking back to his house, and he told us his brother was waiting there with the money, so he could repay my father. That made my father happy. We gave the Negro a lift back to his house.

My father was keen to see inside a house like that, and so we went in. The Negro opened a door, and started yelling horribly. On a bed there was a hideous black woman not moving. That was the Negro's wife. She really and truly was dead, and not a ghost.

The Negro hadn't given the money to the undertakers, he'd spent it on whiskey, to comfort himself. The undertakers said they wouldn't dream of working for nothing. Even though that's just what they did, and twice over. They dug up the woman, and put her back where they'd got her from.

That night we didn't feel like eating anything, but the American people who'd invited us didn't think it was so bad. The only mistake they thought we'd made was in lending money to a Negro and then going to his house.

Before dinner the guests were given big tumblers full of mint leaves and some liquid in the bottom that you're supposed to drink. The whole thing is called a mint julep, and it's a sort of cocktail. My father said it was beyond a joke. Instead of a self-respecting, honest-to-goodness drink, you got given a flowerpot containing a liquid that might be to the liking of the plant that was growing there but was an insult to a grown man. It tasted like sugar water that – at the most – had had a distant view of a whiskey bottle at some stage. Boyhood Friend loved the mint julep and thought it was terribly strong.

In the evening we drove to Ocean View, where we were shown the spot on the coast where the first English settlers landed in America. The water was green and gold with phosphorescence. We toiled up a sand dune and couldn't see much. All the Americans were very moved. My father sighed, because in those days the English hadn't needed a visa to come ashore.

Things got tense, and Boyhood Friend didn't want us around any more. Not one of my father's plans came off. We received no news, just once from the waiter that our borrowed car needed to be returned. I was never able to find out who it belonged to anyway, but it was someone who was a menace right now because he wanted it back.

Where would we sleep? What would we eat? My father

fired off telegrams to Europe that were terribly expensive and didn't help at all. He kept thinking of the terribly rich people we knew in Holland and who were vaguely related to us too. But they didn't like us, and we didn't like them either. They would never give us anything. Why should they?

Then in his desperation my father had an idea, and he thought he would die. He wrote the rich Dutch people a telegram purporting to come from Boyhood Friend, saying that my father had died, and requesting funeral expenses and a crossing for the orphaned girl, which was me. My father said the people would be so happy that he'd died that they would certainly send money, not least to appear magnanimous to the world. The money that came would hardly have buried anyone, but at least it was enough to get us back to New York.

I went swimming for the last time at Virginia Beach. My father said goodbye to the Chinaman who had washed our shirts sometimes, but only those of my father and Boyhood Friend. I always ran around in my bathing costume.

One last time I ran along the beach, further and further. The spidery crabs danced over the sand, the sun shone, the sand glowed. I saw a giant tortoise lying at the water's edge, stinking, and I saw loads of dead fish.

A dark silent mass was approaching the tideline, and I recognized the nuns from St Paul's Hospital, and they got undressed to bathe in private. I was astonished, because I had always thought nuns only consisted of wimples and robes.

In a lonely part of the beach I found a bottle of Gordon's Gin, which my father might have tossed out of the car one night, though maybe it wasn't my father's at all. But it was at that place on the shore where we sometimes parked with Boyhood Friend, because it was Sunday, and the boys and girls drank gin, and the wooded roads echoed with laughter and singing and noise. They were people who had come from the city, in search of peace and quiet.

My father had sought peace and quiet from them, and driven us to the shore, to the dunes. More cars followed us like buzzing beetles, one after another. They stopped in front of us, behind us, next to us. They didn't hoot, we didn't hear them.

They came silently, and stayed, and left silently, and silently new cars took their place. It was like an automobile show, except it wasn't lit, so you didn't get much benefit. I did manage to see something, though, because I secretly crept past some of the cars.

In each car, there was a man and a girl getting all tangled up. My father drank gin, and remarked: 'Love in the USA.' And there was me thinking they were trying to kill each other. One time an older naked man got out of his car, but without wanting to go swimming. He just switched off the headlights of his car.

In the daytime, this remote spot was where nuns went

swimming. I know them because I once spent three days in their hospital. They were very nice to me. I meant to write to them every day from Europe, and they wanted to take me back, and when I said goodbye they blessed me in their little hospital chapel.

The reason I was in their hospital was because in the forest one time I had accidentally sat down on a very interesting and poisonous creeper. That gave me a rash and a high temperature.

When I was almost better, I wandered through the hospital. I wandered in the direction of some very slow gentle singing. I saw a ward that had only sick Negro women in it, and they were doing the slow singing, as if singing a lullaby to the whole world. At their bedsides sat some quiet Negro men. They rolled their eyes in time to the singing of the Negro women.

One of the nurses told my father that almost all these gentle men had thrown their wives out of the window in an argument. That's why the women were in hospital, and by singing they were showing their pleasure at still being alive, and the men were pleased with them. All of them were happy.

Later I wondered with my father whether we shouldn't collect some of the poisonous creepers and pack them into our suitcases for the customs inspectors to touch. But in the end we decided not to, because there are the occasional kind ones, who you have to try to protect.

*

We drove back via Washington, because a boyhood friend of Boyhood Friend's lived there. Our own Boyhood Friend liked us again, because we were leaving. He was also grateful to my father for having saved him from a precipitate marriage.

Washington wasn't a city so much as a cake made of sugar icing and white cream. We were allowed to stay with Boyhood Friend's boyhood friend. His hair was as white as his house and the President's house.

Earlier, he'd used to be a judge, but only sort of on the side. Really he had devoted his entire life to constructing a giant warship made out of buttons. He hadn't permitted himself to buy any of the buttons, they all had to be ones he had either lost or found. He had travelled through Asia and America, and looked for buttons on all the avenues of the world. It took him many years till he had enough buttons, but I think he cheated and sometimes tore buttons off his jackets. I'm sure you never find nice buttons on the prestige streets of the world, because rich people always make sure their buttons are securely sewn on. I said that to the man too. He was a little taken aback, but he did at least say he'd found most of his buttons in places he hadn't wanted to visit.

The button battleship was in a big room made of sea-green velvet. My father and I stood in front of it and gazed at it. The white-haired man walked sadly back and forth. He was proud and tired. He talked and smiled, as if he had already died. He has nothing more to live for now, because the ship is finished. That's what my father said.

In New York, my father managed to sell some stories to a newspaper. That gave him back his appetite for life, and he came round to America again, and believed we would be saved. I went back to Europe on my own to fetch my mother, while my father was going to stay behind and build up a life for us, and send money soon.

I felt tired on the ship, and I had a sore throat, and I couldn't receive any letters. One evening, the captain took me up on the bridge, and I stood miles above the water. I spread out my arms and thought they would get so long that I could reach my father with my left and my mother with the right. Now for the first time, we were all three of us on our own.

How would my father manage to stay in America? Who would he talk to if things got desperate? There isn't anywhere where people like you and tolerate you when things are going badly. And maybe my mother would have starved in Europe before I got back, or died of loneliness.

Now we're all back in Amsterdam together, and one day we'll all be together somewhere else.

'Do you never get homesick?' an old man asked me, and first I didn't know what he meant. He explained.

I do sometimes get homesick, but it's always for different places that I happen to think of. Sometimes I'm thinking of the singing buses on the Côte d'Azur, sometimes of a meadow near Salzburg that was a blue sea of gladioli, of the Christmas trees at my grandmother's house, of the slot machines in New York, of the giant shells in Virginia, and the snow and sleighs carrying straw in Poland.

But I don't want to go anywhere if my mother doesn't come too. It seems I don't really get homesick then. And much less when my father's with us too.

Afterword

I first came to Irmgard Keun by way of the Austrian-Jewish writer Joseph Roth – for all the Roth reasons, if you like. She lived and travelled with him from June 1936 to January 1938, in the middle of her life and at the dog-end of his. (He died in May 1939.) In Joseph Roth biographies, I'd read her very striking and persuasive account of him during those terrible years of exile:

When I first met Roth in Ostende, I felt here was someone who was simply about to die of sadness. His round blue eyes were almost blind with despair, and his voice sounded as though buried under tons of grief. Later on, that impression blurred a little, because at that time Roth wasn't just sad, he was also the greatest and most impassioned of haters . . .

Though always denied by Keun (admittedly, like Roth himself, she was an inveterate liar), the persistent *on dit* is that, at least in part – the generosity, the scrounging, the panache, the drinking, the odd mixture of unreliability and dependability – the character, or perhaps the *circum-stantial character*, of Kully's father, Peter, in *Child of All Nations* is supposed to be based on Roth's. It didn't matter; I ended up so charmed by Keun that I translated the whole book. On the way, I read – much of it aloud – everything else of hers I could find. I suppose it's a little like enjoying your round, and buying the golf course.

Irmgard Keun was born in Berlin in 1905; later, she always claimed it was in 1910, the year her brother Gerd was born. The lie served two purposes: it made her appear younger, and it squashed an upstart rival. (The trauma of the arrival of a younger sibling is introduced, then gently shelved, in *Child of All Nations*.) She grew up in Cologne – where her father worked in the fledgling German petrol industry – and after school took to the stage. For a couple of years she played small parts in provincial rep companies, gaining, it seems, little favour-able notice. She was averagely pretty, shy, willing, and not very good. Defeated as an actress, she began to write in 1929, and here she was immediately successful. She was published right away – in her own hyperbolic account, she was offered a contract within twenty-four hours – and her books sold in the tens of thousands at home, and were translated abroad. She was published by Gallimard in France, and prominently reviewed in the *New York Times* and *The Times Literary Supplement*.

In a sense, impersonation – mimicry – remained the

name of the game. In her early novels, *Gilgi, eine von uns*
('Gilgi, one of us', 1931) and *Das kunstseidene Mädchen*
('The artificial silk girl', 1932), both in the first-person
narrative form that remained most congenial to her,
Keun gave voice to the Young Modern Woman – now
newly and trickily positioned at the crux of work, love
and family – much more effectively than she had been
able to do as an actress in parts written by others. (*Gilgi*
was promptly filmed, the year after it appeared, while a
'Gilgi' as a type of the modern temp soon entered the
language of Weimar Germany.) Keun forms part of the
wonderful efflorescence of women's writing in the 1920s
and 30s – clever, fast-moving, contemporary, important,
and unburdened with the dreary cultural ballast and
the turgid intellectual purpose of so many men's books
of the time – that internationally comprised the likes of
Jean Rhys, Anita Loos, Rosamund Lehmann, Vicki Baum
and later (though she is of their generation, born in
1911) Sybille Bedford. How, Keun's early books ask, can
a young woman ignorant of the German comma laws
hold on to her job (scarce enough commodity in those
times), without letting her boss make free with her calves
(or worse); how in inflationary times and on a small
salary can she afford to buy those few indispensable items
for her wardrobe; how, without becoming a total tramp,
can she have a little fun; how bridge the depressing gulf
between her existence and the women's lives she reads
about in the magazines? Doris's obsession with 'glamour'

(*Glanz* – almost more like 'stardom') in *The Artificial Silk Girl* is cleverly half ironized and half lyrically earnest. She is, as Kathie von Ankum notes in her translation, a predecessor of Bridget Jones and material girls everywhere.

After 1933, things abruptly got much harder for Keun. Now married, and with a husband to feed (the unspeakable Johannes Tralow, theatre director, writer and all-round creature, twenty-three years her elder, an early recruit to the Nazi party, before eventually finding his apotheosis on a ten-pfennig postage stamp in the German Democratic Republic), with a third book on the go that wouldn't behave (*Der hungrige Ernährer*, 'The hungry provider', lost, unfinished, rejected, or most likely all three), she found herself personally, politically and artistically in difficulties. Just as Keun was instinctively anti-Nazi (she would sign letters '*Heil Hittler*' – yes, two t's), so the Nazis were just as instinctively anti-Keun. There was something about her honesty, her spark, her refusal of indoctrination, her subversiveness that riled them more than political opposition. (And, with their emphasis on racial purity and *Familienpolitik* – family values – women were important to them.) In their terms, she was 'immoral' and a writer of '*Asphaltliteratur mit antideutscher Tendenz*' ('urban books' were often thought of as 'discreditable' to Germany for country-sentimental reasons, but also as a handy way of discriminating against their often Jewish authors). Keun was blacklisted, her books removed from bookshops and libraries, and (though she did try later, and rather harder than she would have liked to have done) she was not able to join the *Reichsschrifttumskammer*, the Writers' Union, without which she could not publish or work in Germany.

In 1936, Keun went into exile. Her third novel, her first with a child protagonist, *Das Mädchen, mit dem die Kinder nicht verkehren durften* ('The girl the children weren't allowed to play with'), was published by the Dutch firm of Allert de Lange. A fourth – as good, and again with a young woman, Sanna, at its centre – *Nach Mitternacht*, appeared with Querido in 1937; an English translation, *After Midnight*, came out the following year. In 1938, there was *D-Zug dritter Klasse* ('Express train, third class'), about a compartment full of seven strangers on the train from Berlin to Paris, and in the autumn of 1938 *Kind aller Länder*.

One could, if one had a mind to, follow her movements in those years, via *Child of All Nations*: Ostende first (it was at least a little familiar, because she had holidayed there as a child), Brussels, Amsterdam, Poland, Salzburg, Bordighera in Italy (with her mother), Marseilles, Nice, Paris, America. It is striking that those years, of fear, distraction and worry – the prospect of war looms heavily over *Child of All Nations*, and as something purely destructive, not as the only possible solution to the problem of Hitler – saw her best work. Partly it is the admirable ease with which she wrote, partly the fact that it took work at such a rate simply to pay the bills, but most important, I think, is her exile's sense of mission, the sense that she had in the Nazi regime an antagonist that she needed to wound and puncture. Four books in three years, with constant changes of abode, with the problems of Roth, with her own alcoholism, with the ongoing divorce from Tralow, with another lover, the Jewish doctor Arnold Strauss – to whom she was initially referred in Berlin, for help with her alcoholism – now waiting for her hopefully in Virginia, and receiving regular begging and stalling letters from her.

Following Roth's death, and the uncertainty with Strauss (in May 1938 she finally crossed the Atlantic, as Kully and her father do in *Child of All Nations*, but at the end of eight weeks she crossed back; neither America nor bourgeois life as a doctor's wife were what she was cut out for) and the subsequent invasion of the Netherlands in 1940, she did the oddest thing. She returned to Germany and lived there, semi-legally (she had managed to get a passport issued in the name of Charlotte Tralow), with her parents, in Cologne and on the Rhine. It was a distraction, and no doubt a help, that a mistaken report of her suicide was put about in the English press, but it remains doubtful how she got by. After the war, she wrote humorous and satirical sketches for magazines and the radio, had a child – a daughter, Martina, whom she brought up herself – and wrote one more novel, *Ferdinand, der Mann mit dem freundlichen Herzen*

('Ferdinand, the kind-hearted man'), published in 1950.
Her good, and indeed her great, earlier books were
obscure and out of print, and it was only at the very end
of her life that she was partially rediscovered by a far
younger generation of feminists, including the poet
Ursula Krechel and the Austrian Nobel Prize-winner Elf-
riede Jelinek. I've no doubt that, had she been a man, her
work would have been made available in valorous boxed
sets and collected editions. All in all, it seems a sorry
second half of her life, in and out of hospital for alcohol
and alcohol-related matters. She distinguished herself by
steadfastly refusing to write an autobiography, and died
in 1982, at the age of seventy-seven – or, as she would
have put it, seventy-two.

In the exiled circle in which Keun moved in the mid-to-
late 1930s, she was continually bemused and disappointed
by the chosen subject matter of her peers: 'What are the
other émigrés writing? Kesten has a novel about Philip
II, Roth has one about the Dual Monarchy of Austria-
Hungary, Zweig is writing on Erasmus of Rotterdam,
Thomas Mann on "Lotte in Weimar", Heinrich Mann
on Henri IV, Feuchtwanger on Nero . . . Who is writing
the great book about now?' She is right: more than
ever, it seems like a professional deformation (or at least
dereliction) on the part of her contemporaries. Perhaps
they wanted to assert their independence from day-to-day
politics, accepting (like Roth) the necessity for struggle

in their journalism, but still trying to dream in their novels; certainly, exile internationalized them, and history drew them, because there at least – even as Hitler proclaimed a thousand-year Reich – things still began and ended; or perhaps it was merely their attempt, encouraged by their hard-up émigré publishers, to serve a readership that knew most of the same things they did, and itself craved respite and escape. Who wants to read about Germany now, they must have thought.

Keun has few rivals – I can think of none – as a chronicler of the ambience (in *After Midnight*, which is set in Frankfurt on the day Hitler comes to town) or the consequences (in *Child of All Nations*) of the rise of Nazism. Her canny choice of 'small' central figures, Sanna – the latest off her assembly line of outspoken and straightforward girls in difficult circumstances – and the nine-year-old Kully, allows her to refract and comment on huge themes without using big words; it provides an ideal entry, a shrewd lever. Kully is a wonderful, a purely delightful creation – reminiscent of Kay Thompson's Eloise ('My name is Eloise and I live at the Plaza'), Geoffrey Willans's Molesworth or Richmal Crompton's William, or the real-life nine-year-old Daisy Ashford (author of *The Young Visiters*) – but the really inspired touch is Keun's placing her in the forbiddingly grown-up contexts of dictatorship and exile.

No one who wants to learn about or imagine the German diaspora of the 1930s could do better than pick up *Child of All Nations*. When, following Hitler's coming to power in Germany in 1933, a generation of German writers were turned loose upon the mercy of European exile, they clustered round improvised or adapted periodical- and book-publishing centres in Paris, Amsterdam and Prague. Hundreds lived in the comfortless proximity of Thomas Mann in Sanary-sur-mer in the South of France. ('The malicious village of exile' is the brilliant Auden phrase; as Mann's son-in-law, he may even have had Sanary in mind.) The print-runs – and by inference, the advances – of German-language books printed abroad were one-twentieth of what they had been in Germany. (Joseph Roth had the reputation of being the toughest and most successful bargainer; other authors quickly learned that there was little point in calling on publishers after he had been.) The revelation of Keun is of a lavish existence of hotels and restaurants and first-class travel that kept one imprisoned in a sort of luxurious but penurious bubble. One couldn't afford to break the illusion, say, by making economies, because that would destroy one's credit, and one had no other asset but that credit, and that credit in turn could only be funded by the most shameless and outrageous begging. It seems axiomatic that one could not live and earn money in the same place – wherever one was was either taboo or already skint – and so Peter goes off on his rounds of Europe, leaving wife and child, as they perfectly understand, in pawn. It is a wonderfully formalized machinery:

where one lives wildly beyond one's means, because anything else is so entirely beyond one; where one does either real work for phantom money, or, slightly better, no work for real money; where travel money is used for staying, and staying money pays for travel; it is the institution of the impossible in place of life.

As a child, Kully displays simultaneously the desire to understand, the flexibility to accommodate and the propensity to question; all of which makes her the perfect vehicle for the counter-intuitive world of the literary exile. Hers is a justly peripheral view of a peripheral condition. She is of course far and away the oldest and wisest character in the book – her mother's keeper, her father's agent, way beyond any teacher or policeman or (if they had been invented) social worker in what she knows and how she learns. She knows there are exceptions, but she also knows there are rules. She knows the drawbacks of the free beach as opposed to the paying beach, she knows how to peel prawns faster than her mother, she knows that French is something you can pick up in a morning, she knows (from opening her father's letter to her mother) that 'a novelist shouldn't go all literary in his letters' (which does sound to me like Roth) and she knows from her mother that 'of all the things she needed to know in her life, there was not one that she'd learned at school'. She knows the curious fact that 'books are made in factories as well, but only after they've been written', but then she knows everything there is to know about the writing of them, as witness the fantastic scene with the publisher Herr Krabbe. She is on familiar terms with death, suicide, mental breakdown, hysteria, marital infidelity, international politics ('Hitler belongs to the Germans, but the Italians have one of their own, called Mussolini'), tricks and deceptions of all kinds. She's done things that belong in tall tales: 'The children don't believe me when I say I've been on a sleigh in the Carpathians with my father and a Polish hunter, and have lain on a fur in a hut and eaten bear steaks.' She has an altogether formidable repertoire of alcoholic drinks. She knows that school atlases give a very poor account of the world: 'In reality, all those countries look nothing like that, and most of them I've seen for myself, so I know.' And then – so typical of her – the child's indomitable way of turning a hardship into a badge of distinction: 'And I expect we'll get to see the remaining ones in time too.'

I have one minor quarrel with *Child of All Nations*, which was a delight to translate: I don't like the ending. I don't think Kully should have gone to America. It almost seems like a sequel, tacked on and taken fast. For all that the American passage also ends, becoming not a resolution but one further episode, it breaks the claustrophobia of the book. But then it was always going to be a difficult book to end, following Keun's own movements all the way, as it did. In musical terms, it needs, and gets, a sort of fade-out. I think she would have liked a happy ending (for her own morale, and that of her readers), but that was never a possibility, not for Keun, and not in 1938. (In any case, exile is imprevisible, not a fixed sentence but an open-ended condition.) She did at least scrape past a possible bad ending, with – for the one time in the book – father, mother and Kully each on their own, in three different places, in America, in Europe and on the boat. That, in itself, was a kind of triumph. That they are ever all together again – little brother or no – and making their strange go of things in Holland or wherever, we have to take on trust.

Michael Hofmann
Hamburg
December 2006